The Jayhawkers

Luther Kane, one-time captain with Colonel Mosby's raiders during the Civil War, is forced to leave Texas and lie low in the Nations to avoid bounty hunters tracking down and arresting men who served with the colonel.

He joins up with three Missouri brush boys, outlawed by the Union government and themselves hunted for atrocities they carried out when riding under the black flag of 'Bloody' Bill Anderson.

Now they must take the fight to the red legs in a series of bloody shoot-outs to finally end the war against them.

The Jayhawkers

Elliot Conway

A Black Horse Western

ROBERT HALE · LONDON

ISBN-10: 0-7090-8069-7
ISBN-13: 978-0-7090-8069-5

Robert Hale Limited
Clerkenwell House
Clerkenwell Green
London EC1R 0HT

Typeset by
Derek Doyle & Associates, Shaw Heath
Printed and bound in Great Britain by
Antony Rowe Limited, Wiltshire

In Memory of Wilfred 'Pusser' Hill, ex-RN

ONE

'Rider comin' in fast, Luther,' one of the three-man branding crew said.

Luther Kane, straw boss of the T Star, put the iron back into the fire and loosened the rope on the hog-tied calf, then straightening up his bowed, lean frame eye-balled the dust-raising horseman as the bellowing calf kicked itself to his feet and raced across to its mother.

It had been over nine months since General Robert E. Lee had signed the surrender papers at Appomattox Court House bringing the civil war blood-letting to an end, but the grim stress lines of years of bloody ambush-cades and pitched battles were still etched deep on Luther's hard-boned face.

'It's Lem!' he said, casting a puzzled glance at the ranch hands. 'What the hell is a ranch cook ass-kicking it out here for?'

'M'be that bunch of greaser *bandidos* have sneaked across the Rio Grande again, hopin' to cut out a few dozen longhorns from the south range herd, Luther,' said the ranch hand who had first spotted Lem coming in.

'Could be, Matt. Could well be,' Luther said thought-fully. 'The thieving sonsuvbitches know we haven't got the men to keep a close watch on both herds.'

Shortage of good drovers and ranch hands was another factor ageing Luther's face. During the war years with most Texan males fighting hundreds of miles north of the Lone Star State, as far north as the slaughterhouse of the battle of Gettysburg, the herds of longhorns had multiplied in their thousands. Too many to handle for the Texans who had been fortunate enough to survive all the killings and still possessed all their limbs to be able to sit up on their horses and work cattle.

Hard men, gringos, Mexicans and Apache were able to lift ranchers' stock whenever they had the need to do so. Rustlers or not, whatever message Lem was bringing to him seemed urgent. It was a long time ago since Luther had seen the cook up on a horse, let alone a mount under the whip. Lem's normal pace for moving around was as fast as the chuck wagon, hauled by an ancient mule, could roll across the plain.

Lem, still wearing his once white cook's apron, yanked his horse into a haunch-touching dirt halt. 'Two fellas showed up at the big house, Luther,' he said, still in his saddle. 'Askin' for you! They were a coupla Yankee bounty-hunter sonsuvbitches. They showed the boss the papers they were holdin' on one Captain Luther Kane, dead or alive papers. Bein' that you were one of Colonel Mosby's murderous scum. Their words not mine, Luther,' Lem added apologetically.

'The boss told them you were out working on the south range,' continued Lem. 'He also told them that Southern hospitality allowed them one visit to the T Star ranch but if they ever showed up on his front stoop agin he'd treat them as trespassers and personally blast

THE JAYHAWKERS

them to hell where they belonged with his shotgun.
After they rode out to the south range the boss told me
to get out here fast and warn you of the situation. Told
me to tell you that you had to get outa Texas pronto
like. M'be ride north to the Nations till the bastards get
tired of tryin' to hunt you down.' Lem then loosed the
roped-on bundle at the back of his saddle and, along
with a small roll of dollar bills, handed it down to
Luther. 'That's all your gear I could gather up, Luther,
and the cash is your due, plus a little extra to tide you
over till you come back.'

Luther cursed. He knew that Colonel Mosby's
command, like the other reb irregular units, Quantrill's
and 'Bloody' Bill Anderson's brush boys, hadn't been
included in the surrender terms. Their way of fighting
the war, burning out peaceful communities, shooting
and killing non-combatants, was condemned by both
Union and Confederate Governments but Luther hadn't
thought that the Yankee hatred against them would have
reached this far south and for so long after the end of the
war for blood money men to be on his trail.

He did some more cursing. What the hell did Jeff Davis
sitting there in his fine presidential house at Richmond
know what kind of war was being fought up there along
the backwoods of the Kansas–Missouri border country.
The killing there had been going on longways before the
Confederacy broke away from the Union and started the
big killing war. The guerillas fought under the black flag,
the take-no-prisoners, no-surrender banner. Under those
conditions, Luther thought, things were bound to get out
of hand, folk killed who shouldn't have been. But that was
what war was all about, killing. And Colonel Mosby's

9

command sure did that.

'Thank's, Lem,' he said, as he strapped his gear on to his own horse and mounted up. 'And thank the boss for the extra cash. Tell him I'll come south in about a month's time to see how the situation is. I figure those Yankee bounty-hunters won't stay long hereabouts if they're not going to earn their blood money at the T Star.' Luther grinned at his branding crew. 'I'm sorry I have to leave you boys to finish off here, but as you heard the boss said I've got to quit Texas and you know he expects his orders to be carried out.'

'You git, Luther,' Matt replied. His leathery face cracked in a smile. 'Cookie there can give me and Lafe a hand. What he dishes up for us hard-workin' hands don't take long to fix.'

'If the Yankee sonsuvbitches come by this way askin' their nosy questions,' Lafe said, 'We'll tell them you're across the border into New Mexico tryin' to rope in some cows that have strayed across the Rio Grande.' He grinned at Luther. 'Just watch yourself in the Nations; I've heard it's a wild and wide open territory.'

Luther grinned back at him as he dug his heels into his mount. 'And Texas isn't?'

His horse set off at a steady easy trot heading for the Panhandle and the Nations border. Where distance and time, he hoped, would rid him once and for all of the Yankee blood hunters.

He had hardly lost sight of the branding camp when, for no apparent reason other than a puzzling uneasiness, Luther halted his mount. He took a good look all around him, but could see nothing that should have caused his nerves to twitch. But living by his old wartime maxim, to always be prepared for the worst, he reached behind him and pulled out a lightweight .32 Colt pistol from his bedroll and pushed it down the top of his right boot. He wouldn't be able to walk very far with it stuck down there but it could come in handy if his uneasiness was more than just nerves. Could be the difference between living or dying.

Culley, a tall, thin, hollow-cheeked man smiled a death's head grin at his partner.

'I told you that Texican rancher was tryin' to lead us on a wild goose chase, Wes. That's our bird comin' along the trail, or my name ain't Culley Jones.'

The two bounty-hunters were bellied down behind a slight ridge close to the trail, their rifles laid out in front of them, shells levered in the firing chambers.

They had received a hostile-eyed reception from the rancher and after telling them that the man they were seeking was branding on the south range, he had warned them that if they showed up on his land again they would end up dead.

Culley had taken the threat in po-faced silence though he had a burning urge to do some shooting down himself, just to show the old bastard who had won the war. What him and Wes were doing was legal work and they had papers to prove it, but it was eat-crow time. They had travelled this far to be able to collect a sizeable bounty, not to get full of Texas lead.

Hard-eyeing the rancher just to show that no no-good ex-reb could intimidate him, he tugged at Wes's sleeve. 'It seems that we ain't welcome here, pard; let's be on our way and pick up Mr Luther Kane.'

He didn't know how Wes was feeling, but he was sweating blood as they stepped off the porch and walked the few yards to their horses, expecting at any moment the two hatchet-faced ranch hands standing at the far end of the porch would yank out their long-barrelled hand cannons and cut loose at them.

One thing he knew for sure, Culley thought, as he swung up on to his horse, if Kane was working on this south range, wherever that stretch of grass was in this Godforsaken, sun-baked territory, he'd kiss the rancher's ass and apologize to him for thinking he was a liar. Once out of sight of the ranch house Culley told Wes to swing round back aways so that they could keep a watch on the house.

'That Texan bastard was lyin' through his teeth, Wes,' he said. 'That ex-raider ain't out in this direction at all, but if we keep an eye on the house, I've more than a gut feelin' we'll soon find out his whereabouts.'

Pulling up their horses in the shelter of a stand of thickly leafed timber, the pair were just in time to see a ranch hand mount a horse and ride out, westwards.

Culley grinned his grimace of a smile. 'Now why would the cook be raisin' the dirt, Wes? It ain't likely he's in a hurry to get to the sutler's because he's run outa flour and sowbelly, is it?'

Wes flashed a humourless smile of his own. 'That rancher don't know it, but he's pointed us to the capt'n, though in a roundabout way.'

Luther's uneasiness suddenly became dangerous reality as he heard a crack of a rifle and the hiss of a shell passing close by him. He had ridden blindly into an ambush set by the two bounty-hunters! He knew it was no use making a grab for his rifle. The man up on the high ground to his left had him well and truly fixed in his sights and could have opened up with a killing shot if that had been his purpose. They wanted him alive and he wanted to stay that way as long as he could. Alive he had the chance, as slim as it looked right now, to turn the tables on the bounty-hunters. Rigid in the saddle, his hands both raised high, it was waiting-for-a-break time.

Only one man showed himself on the ridge, which caused Luther some extra fretting. If the second bounty-hunter was bellied down somewhere to his right then the bastards had him between them. He was hoping to get the wild chance of shooting two men dead before either of them put paid to him. To do that, both men had to be real close together and he would have to fire fast and true. He would have no time to gun down men on either side of the trail.

'You keep a bead on the capt'n, Wes,' Luther heard the man on the ridge call over his shoulder. 'While I go down and get his guns off him!'

As the bounty-hunter picked his way down the grade Luther saw the other ambusher come into view on the ridge, his rifle up to his shoulder. The pair were together! Luck was beginning to swing his way.

Culley, rifle held loosely, stopped several feet from Luther and grinned up at him. 'Just unbuckle your gunbelt and drop it to the ground, Capt'n,' he said. 'Then do likewise with your Winchester.' Culley's smile faded and his grip on his rifle tightened. 'Nice and easy, Capt'n. Any crazy move like tryin' a wild-ass shoot-out and Wes up there will plug you dead and we'll haul you back to the nearest army fort in the Nations tarp-wrapped across the back of your horse. It don't matter which way to us, the warrant out on you 'as got "dead or alive" writ on it. Though you'll be stinkin' to high heaven if we have to shoot you before we make it to the Nations, kinda unsettlin' for the horses.'

Luther, as tensed up as a hound dog in heat, did as he had been ordered and his pistol belt, followed by his Winchester thudded on the ground by the side of his horse.

'You can come on down, Wes!' Culley yelled. 'The capt'n ain't goin' to cause us any trouble. We can get him roped up and get to hell outa this reb country before any of the capt'n's *amigos* show up and take a spoilin' hand in our business.'

Luther shot a hawk-eyed glance at the second bounty-hunter coming down on to the trail, trying to keep poker-faced. Bounty-hunters by their nature were hair-triggered nervy men and if they saw as much as a gleam of defiance in his eyes they'd shoot him dead. He was about to play his wild card in a game he would never get a second deal at the cards.

Both of the bounty-hunters were within close shooting range of him, relaxed, rifles lowered, smiling at the ease with which they had jumped him.

'You just step down, Capt'n,' Culley said, 'so Wes can truss you up.'

Luther swung out of his saddle with his left leg in the stirrup iron, his right leg and the booted gun on the blind side of the bounty-hunters. When he turned from his mount and faced them the gun was out and firing.

The first shot hammered through Culley's skull

killing him dead in an instant. Wes, shot twice in the chest, lived long enough to show an agony-twisted face before he fell lifeless alongside his partner. Luther pushed the death-dealing pistol down the top of his pants. It seemed, he thought morbidly, his killing days hadn't ended. He bent over and picked up his gunbelt and rifle.

Ten minutes later he was slapping the rumps of the bounty-hunters' horses, their late owners lying face down across their saddles, to send them trotting off in the direction of the branding camp. The boys would know what to do with the bodies and the horses. No Texas peace officer would bring charges against him for the killings. A one against two shoot-out, with both losers showing frontal wounds, would be classed as jusified self-defence by any Texas jury. With the dead men being Yankee blood-money men, Luther reckoned that the townsfolk would want him to run for mayor.

But there could be more bounty hunters snooping around the county and it was wise to do what his boss had suggested, hide out in the Nations for a spell. He had dealt successfully with one threat he had been forced to face, it wasn't good thinking to stay in Texas and risk another confrontation with hired killers, as he might not be so lucky next time. He mounted up and started off on his journey again, accepting the cold hard fact that the war was not yet over for him.

TWO

Luther's horse almost stepped on to the camp-fire. The faint blaze of a trail he was following through the tangle of canyons hoping it would lead him out on to the flat, took a dog leg turn to the left, then directly in front of him on the sandy bank of a shallow stream was the camp. With a muttered oath he tugged sharply on the reins before his horse scattered the burning branches and the battered, smoke-blackened coffee pot resting in the glowing embers. The two alarmed-faced men squatting at the fire kicked sand high as they scrambled frantically to their feet, hands reaching for holstered pistols.

Luther raised both hands high. 'Hold it, boys!' he called out. 'I'm not looking for trouble! All I'm seeking is a way out of this rocky wilderness! I've heard there's a town of sorts somewhere north of here, that's if I've calculated right, and I'm out of Texas and riding in Indian Territory.'

'You've calculated rightly, mister.' It was the burlier of the two men who spoke, a bearded, furtive-eyed man. As he was, Luther thought wryly. 'You've made it to the

Nations and that town you're seekin' ain't but a coupla hours' ride along this here crick. Tampas, they call it though some folk wouldn't call that dog-dirt collection of shacks and soddies a town. The only law here in the Nation's no mans land is what a fella carries.' The big man tapped the heavy pistol stuck in the top of his pants. The big man's lips twitched in a sort of a smile. 'I reckon that information should interest you, mister. Though it ain't no business of me and my pard's to wonderin' why a fella instead of takin' the main trail north to the Nations picks himself a wolf's trace through this rough country to get where he's headin' for.'

Luther gimlet-eyed the big man. 'You're right, friend, it isn't any of your business.' He switched his gaze on the big man's partner, taking in the faded and much stained grey tunic the small man was wearing. 'Being nosy myself,' he said, 'I'm figuring you're both ex-rebs.'

Both men stiffened up and their hands strayed towards pistol butts.

The little man spoke for the first time. 'Yeah, we fought for the South,' he said in a flat, hard voice. 'Does that upset you any?'

'If you gents are making for Texas,' replied Luther, 'why, every man you meet on the trail will be an ex-reb.' He grinned. 'Now if it was any business of mine I'd ask why the pair of you are sneaking into Texas by the back door.'

The two men exchanged glances and by their looks Luther guessed they had come to some agreement. The little man addressed him again.

'Me and Chas,' he began, 'were Jayhawkers, rode with Colonel William Quantrill way up there in Missouri and Kansas.' The little man spat in the fire. Now me and Chas rightly thought that bein' we had shed blood for the Confederate cause, many of the boys we rode with gave their lives for the South, we'd be welcomed home with open arms, kinda like ragged-assed heroes, able to get on ploughin' and plantin' our land.' The little man's face worked in anger as he spat in the fire again. 'Then we found out that the Goddamned blue bellies wanted to hang us for bein' no better than low down murderers! Worse killers than bronco Injuns! When my pard said that a man's gun is the only law to this part of the Nations it's because the local town sheriffs and the few state marshals servin' warrants for "Hangin'" Judge Parker back there in Fort Smith, Arkansas, ain't doin' damn all to stop Colonel Lane's red legs from ridin' across the territory actin' as regulators. Those bastards have burnt out families they believed had been shelterin' and feedin' us brush boys, now they're on our trail.' The small man eyed Luther. 'Mister, if you want to keep livin' in this neck of the Nations, don't whistle "Dixie".'

'Well I'll be damned!' Luther said. 'I could be jumping out of the skillet into the fire if I don't watch my step. I was a captain with Colonel Mosby's raiders and though we were a regular army outfit the blue bellies didn't like the rough ways we waged war. And like you Missouri guerillas they weren't keen to take any of us prisoner. Two bounty-hunters came down into Texas carrying papers for my arrest so the Union could put me on trial for breaking the rules of war by causing unnecessary civilian casualties.'

'Just like Colonel Lane's night riders did to Southern sympathizers,' interrupted the little man.

Luther thin-grinned. 'The winners of a war can make their own rules, friend. Thanks for the warning. At least unlike the two blood-money men who were on my trail those red legs don't hold any warrants on me, but as I said, I'll walk quietly if I ever come close to any of them.'

'Are those bounty-hunters comin' along your back trail, Capt'n?' the big raider asked. 'Me and my pard ain't got any pressin' business in Texas so if we meet up with a coupla fellas with shifty-eyed looks of bounty-hunters trailin' north we could kinda delay them somewhat.' He grinned at his partner. 'Aint' that so, Jess?'

'We sure can, Chas,' Jess replied. 'It's beholden on us ex-raiders to help each other out.'

Luther smiled. 'There's no need to put yourselves out any, *amigos,* I've already delayed them, permanently. The pair got over confident and got themselves dead.' Luther touched the brim of his hat in a farewell gesture. 'Now it's time I rode out if I want to make it to Tampas before dark. You'll be OK in Texas. Texans have always been rebels. General Santa Anna found that out to his cost. Colonel Lane's boys won't risk showing their noses south of the Nations.' He smiled again. 'My apologies for spilling your coffee and interrupting your meal.'

With 'Good luck' cries from the two jayhawkers sounding in his ears Luther gave his horse its head and at a steady high-stepping pace it pounded its way along the edge of the creek.

THREE

Luther rode slowly along Main Street, Tampas, wondering how he was going to earn his keep until he opined it was safe enough for him to return to the T Star. The money he had with him would tide him over for a couple of weeks, if he only used it for essentials and kept out of the saloons, otherwise he would end up being the town bum. He didn't know if there were any cattle spreads hereabouts; working cattle was all he knew, that and killing, he thought grimly. He decided that the nearest saloon would be the place to find out if any rancher was signing men on, and the cheapest rooming-house.

The sun was just past its height and, apart from him, the only other movement on the street was caused by swirling heat-raised dust devils, though Luther saw that six horses were tied up outside a saloon on the wind-swinging sign of which he picked out the paint faded name. The Wild Hog. He drew up his mount outside the saloon.

As he was tethering his horse to the hitching rail, Luther ran a casual-eyed gaze over the horses and expertly judged that they were not part of a ranch's *remuda* as all their saddle gear was new. Looking closer at the nearest mount, he noticed that it had the letters US branded on its flank. And he remembered the jayhawkers' warning about Yankee red-legs being in the territory. He pushed open the saloon doors and also remembered his promise to walk lightly if he met up with any of the Yankee irregulars.

Two of the red-legs were drinking at the bar, one of them a heavily built man who had sergeant's chevrons on his tunic sleeves; the other four were sitting at a nearby table playing cards. All of them wore regular US army tunics but they favoured their own style in pants: buckskins, cords and store-bought broadcloth. The sergeant wore soft red leather knee-high boots, a genuine red leg.

Another thing Luther noticed that set them apart from regular Yankee horse soldiers was that instead of the normal reload pouches strapped on their pistol belts they had a bandolier of brass shells slung across the shoulders and chest, and, as he'd had when he rode with Mosby, some of them had an extra pistol stuck in the waistband of their pants. Shut-faced men who had to be taken seriously.

Luther was conscious of six suspicious, hard-eyed stares as he bellied up to the bar and ordered a beer, but he kept his own eyes off the red legs. The barkeep, a thin-shouldered man, had the same unsettled features as he had. It seemed that he wasn't overjoyed at having Union manhunters drinking in his bar.

Luther carried his beer across to a table next to one occupied by two elderly citizens and sat down, keeping his back to the red legs. He nodded a greeting to the two old-timers but got no acknowledgement in return. Luther guessed that they had heard his Texas drawl when he had ordered his beer, and Texicans being natural born rebels, didn't want to be seen to be having any friendly feelings towards him. The red legs, Luther thought, even when they were not hanging suspected ex-reb brush boys, were still a threatening presence. He could understand the two jayhawkers he had met on the trail having the urge to leave the Nations. This close to a bunch of red legs was putting the fear of God in him.

Bounty-hunters did their work for the blood money and could cease their hunting if the odds went against them; the red legs hunted down ex-reb brush boys because they believed that it was their God-given right to despatch to hell suchlike scum, and only a killing shot would stop them doing that task.

Luther was about to go to the bar for another beer when he heard the bar doors swinging open behind him then footsteps striking hard on the planking floor. He risked a quick glance over his shoulder at the saloon's new customer, a youngish, but gaunt-faced Union Army officer, complete with sabre swinging at his right hip. His left eye was covered by a black eye-patch and Luther saw that, as he walked, his right leg swung out in an awkward swinging gait. Like the sergeant he wore red-leg boots.

Before the war had ended, Captain Paul Chartris had lived with a big chip on his shoulder, a fearsome hatred against the reb guerilla fighters. As second lieutenant in a regular cavalry regiment he had distinguished himself at the bloody killing fields of Sharpsburg, winning his captain's bars and command of a company of cavalry charged with clearing the backwoods of Missouri of the remnants of Quantrill and 'Bloody' Bill Anderson's guerilla bands.

The captain soon discovered it was a different kind of war he had to fight. No blood-racing cavalry charges, sabre flashing, guidons flapping, at a line of ragged-assed reb infantry. Combat in the dank thickets and timber stands was the territory of ambushcades. A sudden, unexpected burst of gunfire, and several troopers lying dead, then the rapidly fading sound of horses crashing through the undergrowth, long before he could rally his men to take up the pursuit of the guerrillas.

One such bloody mêlée had left him part crippled, part blinded and when he had been declared fit enough to return to duty having a game leg and minus an eye, his days of hell or glory charges were over and he had to accept a posting to the non-combative commissariat service. The captain hadn't hated the rebs, they were fighting for what they thought was right, as he was doing, and if he been killed in some regular battle, so be it, but to have been crippled by a bunch of ragged-assed, unshaven, white trash in some penny-ante skirmish galled him more than somewhat. He despised the reb irregulars with a hatred that burnt as fiercely as the late John Brown's hatred for the pro-slavers had been.

Then the captain heard of a Colonel Lane who commanded a regiment that took on the reb guerillas on their own territory and in their own style of killing and applied for a posting to the colonel's outfit, willing to drop rank to an enlisted man if needs be, so determined was he to get back to fighting the brush boys of Missouri.

At his interview with Colonel Lane the captain explained how his wounds had prevented him from rejoining his regiment. And that he was not minded to see the war out working as a quartermaster's clerk. He would be willing to risk falling off his horse to get back into action again.

'Captain,' Colonel Lane said, 'as long as you're keen to shoot down those no-good reb murderers I'll make sure you stay in your saddle myself!'

Over the months that followed along the Missouri–Kansas pro-reb border country, the one-eyed blue-belly captain was as feared for his bloodthirsty ruthlessness as the free-staters of Lawrence, Kansas, once feared Quantrill's raiders. The captain had become a full-blooded red leg.

After the war he volunteered to command a special unit of red legs with wide-ranging authority to hunt down named rebs who had once fought with Quantrill or 'Bloody' Bill Anderson's marauders with the purpose of bringing them to trial, to face charges of murder and destruction of property under the pretence of carrying out military operations. Many of the ex-rebs who were roped in by the red-leg vigilantes didn't make it to the military courts. They were given a few minutes to babble out a short final prayer before the hanging rope was slipped around their necks. Freshly dug graves sprouted widely along the backwoods trails in territory once the stamping ground of the reb guerillas. Kansas and Missouri had been cleared of the last of the Southern hold-outs and the captain and his hunting pack had moved south, into the Nations, to attempt to pick up the trail of fugitives who were still running free.

Luther heard the scraping of chairs, bottles and glasses clinking, as men got to their feet with some haste. The Yankee officer must have something going for him, Luther thought; he looked only half the age of the men he commanded, but they moved smartly in his presence although they hadn't the cut of regular cavalry troopers.

'Sergeant Barker!' he heard the officer call out. 'We're moving out in twenty minutes! See to it that the men have five days' rations, horses likewise!'

'Right, Capt'n,' the sergeant snapped back. 'Murphy, Coster, you heard the capt'n, see to it! The rest of you round up the troop. We'll form up outside!'

After the men had clattered out of the saloon to carry out the sergeant's orders Luther heard the sergeant ask the captain where they were heading for.

'I've received intelligence that there's been a sighting of several of Colonel Mosby's former guerillas, men on a par with Quantrill's killers, in a town called Willow Creek. The man who can identify them is waiting for us outside town.' Captain Chartrist gave a ghost of a smile. 'He fears his life would be in danger if seen consorting with red legs. We haven't any of Colonel Mosby's men on our list, Sergeant, but they deserve the same fate as the other back-shooting scum we've hunted down.'

Luther could hardly prevent himself from yanking out his pistols and gunning down the red-leg officer at

25

hearing that men who could have been in his outfit were to be hunted down like mad dogs. And the son-of-a-bitch Yankee was enjoying doing it! As long as men like Chartris still carried all that hatred around for ex-rebs, Luther thought bitterly, the war would never be over.

Luther's face hardened in grim determined lines. If the war was still being fought then it was time he took part in it. His skulking along back trails biding his time until it was safe to go back to Texas was over. His first action in the extended war the red legs were fighting would be to warn the men at Willow Creek of their danger.

Luther waited a couple of minutes or so after the red-leg captain and his men left the saloon before getting up from the table and crossing over to the bar. Taking a chance that he had read right the barkeep's low opinion of the red legs, he said, 'Friend, like you, I'm not full of brotherly love regarding those Yankee manhunters, so I would be obliged if you could point me in the direction of that Willow Creek the one-eyed captain spoke of. Fellas I fought alongside could be there and I figure it's beholden on me to warn them of the trouble coming their way.'

The barkeep gave Luther a quick assaying look before he answered. 'Follow the east bank of the Cimarron. You'll pick up the river on the north trail outa town. An hour's hard ridin' and you'll raise Willow Creek, a dead dog burg. It's an old silver mining town, but the silver's long played out. There's still a few idiots scratchin' at the dirt up there hopin' for a miracle to hit them by findin' another motherlode before they're forced to eat grass to stay alive. If your buddies are at Willow Creek they'll be up on the high ground lookin' for paydirt; there ain't any other payin' work up there.'

Luther thanked the barkeep for the information and turned to walk out of the bar. Before he had reached the door one of the old-timers called out, 'Ride hard, son. Those red legs m'be sonsuvbitches, but they can ass-kick it around as speedily as any of Fitzroy Lee's Light Horse boys.'

Luther halted, turned and grinned at him. 'Colonel Mosby's boys weren't sluggards on the trail either, *amigo.*' He pushed open the door and stepped down on to the street and unhitched his horse as the first of the rousted red legs came along Main Street leading their horses.

FOUR

Willow Creek wasn't a ghost town yet. It still had a general store with its windows not boarded up and a saloon open to serve liquor to the ranch hands from the nearby cattle spreads who rode into town on pay days, and the dozen or so 'hoping for a miracle' miners still digging at the workings of the abandoned silver mine.

The mine had once been a going concern, employing over 150 miners on round-the-clock shifts, and Willow Creek a wide-open, rip-roaring boom town, boasting twelve saloons and two bawdy houses to relieve the miners of their hard-come-by wealth as painlessly as possible.

Then the motherlode ran out and what showing of silver there was left in the mine wasn't worth the expensive outlay to dig it out, so the mine's Eastern owners closed it down. The miners moved out to seek work elsewhere, the saloon owners, the bawdy-house madams and the storekeepers did likewise hoping to find another booming mining town. A few diehards did stay behind to work the old seams, desperate, thin-faced, deep-set-eyed men hoping that their lifelong ill-starred luck would change and their swinging picks would uncover a streak of paydirt, enough for them to quit mining before the ball-aching grind saw them dead.

Four such-like seekers of their fortunes weren't regular miners but were as gaunt-faced and empty-bellied as the real stay-behind miners; hard-done-by-feeling men since before the end of the war, and more so since its ending. The men had served under Colonel Mosby in one of his hard-hitting cavalry regiments, raiding guerilla fashion, a long way behind the Union lines. Once the killing and the burning out had ended, they had returned to their farms to see their families once more and to catch up with the years of neglect their growing land had suffered in their absence, only to discover that although the war had officially ended, Colonel Lane's red-leg irregulars were still fighting it by burning their homes and barns. They were forced to seek shelter with anyone whose sympathy for the now lost rebel cause was stronger than the dread of the night-riding red legs and the fearful retribution they meted out to any settlers who gave succour to any of Colonel Mosby's guerilla fighters. It was settling time of old hatreds for the red legs.

Not wanting to inflict more pain and suffering on their kinfolk, they didn't make it their business to find out which of their so-called neighbours pointed them out as reb irregulars to the red legs and deal with the dirty stinking turncoats; instead they shook the dust of Missouri off their horses' hoofs and rode south and west into the lawless no-man's land of the Nations.

Even if the fugitives had been cattlemen they knew it

would be dangerous to seek work on any of the few ranches they had passed. Although they had heard that there wasn't much red-leg activity in the Nations they were here, and cattle spreads would be the likeliest places they would check for suspected rebs.

They made it safely to Willow Creek without being challenged by a Union patrol, red leg or regular blue-bellies, and saw the derelict mine and several men working at the face of the black rock butte. Taking it that the old mine must still hold some of its pay dirt, they dropped stakes there, though they calculated by the ragged state of the men who were looking for it they wouldn't get rich. But it was a place to lie low until the day Colonel Lane's red-leg killers were disbanded and real peace came to the former soldiers of the South.

Luther made good time to Willow Creek and, twist-ing in his saddle, he looked along his back trail, a long clear view, into the far distance, and could see no signs of the dust of a bunch of hard-pressing riders. So far so good, he thought. Now all he had to do was to find where Mosby's men were and tell them the bad news.

Just ahead of him the trail divided, the left-hand fork ran to the town, and even at this distance he could see that Willow Creek was a played out place, with boarded-up stores and a deserted Main Street. The track leading up the slope to the mine was steep and overgrown with sagebrush and grass, deeply rutted by the passage of once heavily loaded wagons. Luther could see the broken-timbered hauling gear and several upturned mine trucks lying alongside it. The mine seemed as empty of activity though he heard the sounds of picks striking rock and saw the wisps of smoke from several camp-fires. There were men up there and men could be asked questions. And they would have to be quickly asked. Ominous dust clouds could be appearing along the trail at any time. All he had to hope for was that he got quick answers back. He knee'd his horse up the track.

Only one man, a shaggy-bearded, dirt-encrusted individual, wearing clothes a town's bum would be hard put to wear, was sitting at the first camp-fire he came up to, watching a fire-smoked blackened can of water coming to the boil. The legs of another man were protruding out of a hole in the butte face several yards away and Luther heard the sound of a wielded pick.

The man at the fire looked up at him and Luther felt immediately he had struck lucky. The man's gaze had a hard, wary look about it, as though he had more chewing away at his guts than the hope of striking it rich. And although he had never met any silver miners before, having a long-barrelled Colt Dragoon pistol nestling in a flapped cavalry holster didn't seem one of the tools of their trade. Luther gave one last apprehensive glance over his shoulder, the trail was still clear, then he looked directly at the miner.

'Mister,' he said, 'there isn't time for me to make small talk so all I want to say is that if you know where the ex-rebs who served in Colonel Mosby's outfit are on this hillside I'd be obliged if you'd warn them that there's a troop of red legs led by a one-eyed captain heading this way from Tampas to round them up. And the captain has a fella riding with him who knows the rebs.'

Luther froze in the saddle as he heard the blood-chilling double click of a Winchester being loaded behind him. Then a voice said, 'Just who the hell are you, mister?'

Luther risked a look round. A man was standing on a boulder covering him with his rifle. He swung his gaze back on to the man at the fire. He was on his feet now and his big pistol was out of its sheath and aimed at him. And the man whose legs he had seen was standing out in the open with a pistol fisted.

The man holding the rifle spoke again. 'He smells like a stinkin' bounty-hunter to me, boys,' he growled, gimlet-eying Luther.

'You've got every right to be suspicious of me,' Luther said, keeping his hands well clear of his guns. 'But if I was a blood-money man do you think I'd be so loco to go up against three of Colonel Mosby's raiders on my ownsome?'

'Four raiders, mister.' Another voice and another gun aimed at him as a fourth man pushed his way clear of a patch of brush.

Luther grinned. 'Then I'd be real crazy to try throw down on you all.' His smile faded. 'As I said, time is running out for you boys, there'll be a bunch of red legs pounding along that trail soon, take my word for it. I'm a Texan, Luther Kane, I was captain of a cavalry troop in the 1st Missouri Volunteers.' He grinned again. 'We reckoned we were the best horse-soldier boys Colonel Mosby had. As an old raider I judged it my duty to warn you of the big trouble coming your way. I'm on the run myself, though not from Colonel Lane's butchers. A couple of bounty-hunters tried to jump me back there in Texas; their blood-money hunting days are over, but just in case any more of the sonsuvbitches are prowling around I'm keeping well clear of my part of Texas for the time being.'

'Capt'n Kane, you said, of the 1st Volunteers?' the man at the fire said. 'Did you know a Buck Madison?'

Luther laughed. 'None better! That old whiskey soak was my top sergeant. He got badly wounded in the bloody skirmish we had with half a brigade of Union cavalry at Grant's Crossing. Bad enough to get him invalided out of the army. I haven't heard any news of him since.'

'Buck's dead, Capt'n,' the ex-raider replied. 'A coupla months after the war a bunch of red legs raided his cabin and burnt the place down while he was asleep in his bed. The red-leg sonsuvbitches would do likewise to us if they could, that's why we're livin' here like wild critters.' He cold smiled. 'And by the look of us you can see it ain't been much of a livin'. But it's better than havin' a noose slipped around your neck or doin' a life stretch in a Yankee jail. Now by what you've told us we'll have to pull up stakes here and find another hole to crawl into.'

'How did you find out about the red legs bein' on our trail, Capt'n?' the man who had been working in the hole asked.

'I walked into a bar back there in Tampas,' replied Luther. 'And there they were, six of the bastards. Then in marched their captain, a youngish fella with a patch over his left eye who walked favouring his right leg, so he had been well blooded. By the way he talked to his men he still held a real hatred for us rebs. I heard him tell his sergeant to round up the rest of his troop as he'd had information that some former reb guerillas were working in Willow Creek. And that he was taking a man with him who could point out the rebs to him.'

'It must have been one of those miners workin' on the west face, boys,' the man at the fire said. 'We heard one of them was quittin' the diggin's. He must have heard us talkin' about the old days and decided to earn himself some easy-come-by cash by sellin' us out to the red legs.' He grinned up at Luther. 'By what you've told us it looks as thought there ain't the time to ask you to step down and partake of some coffee with us, Capt'n.'

'Not unless we want to fight a smaller version of Grant's Crossing,' replied Luther. 'I've got to move as well. That red-leg captain saw me in that bar and if he claps eyes on me here in Willow Creek and the fellas he's hunting are gone, he'll have more than a suspicion that I had something to do with their disappearance. And as I said, I judge him to be an unforgiving sonuvabitch to any ex-Mosby man.'

'Anyway, thanks for warnin' us, Capt'n,' the Missourian behind Luther said. 'You can be on your way. Me and the boys will be off this hill in no time at all. We were allus slick movers, the colonel saw to that. Nowadays we're a tad faster bein' that we're travellin' lighter.' His face hardened. 'But there's one job that wants seein' to before we quit this hell of a land.'

Luther was going to ask what the job was but reckoned it was the ex-raider's business not his. Instead he said, 'If you swing wide of those sonsuvbitches who are coming up the trail you'll make it to Texas in a few hours.' He grinned. 'Ex-rebs won't go hungry in Texas, but you may have to keep a watchful eye open for sneaky-looking *hombres* who could be bounty-hunters. You won't have to worry about the captain trailing you. The sight of a bunch of red legs riding across Texas soil would have the whole State raring to start up the war again.'

Luther dismounted while the four gathered up their gear and, as he had been told, it didn't take long to have it strapped on the backs of their horses. Then there were handshakes all round and mutual 'Good lucks' exchanged between them.

The man who had been at the fire said he was called Lucius Cambell, an ex-sergeant and unofficial leader of the band. 'That big fella who was sweatin' his balls off in that hole,' he told Luther, 'is called Des Warner. Him totin' that big Sharps gun is Jake Smith. He was the crackshot of the regiment and believe me there were some pretty fancy shooters in the outfit. Jake, given a fair wind, could down a man for keeps at nine hundred yards with that cannon, or hit him sorely enough for the fella to be of no use to himself or anyone else for the rest of his natural. The mournful-lookin' character is Jake's brother,' continued Lucius. 'He's our quarter-master, sees to it that we eat more or less regularly.' He grinned. 'You can see by the look of us he don't overfill us. Now it's time we boys were movin' out and do what we're beholden to do then we'll head for Texas as you suggest, Capt'n. M'be we'll have the pleasure of meetin' up with you again.'

'That could well happen, Lucius,' replied Luther. 'I don't intend to stray too far away from Texas for any length of time. Though I'll have to move further north before the red-leg captain shows up here at Willow Creek.'

He watched the four Missourians ride down on to the flat, four ragged-assed, hunted men who had been disowned by the government they had shed blood for. Yet still maintained enough of the true grit that had served them well through the hell of war to not to give up their freedom. He saw them cut away from the trail then quickly lost sight of them in the thickly timbered ground to the east of the trail. He rode down from the mine and took the short trail to Willow Creek, only stopping long enough to water his mount at a horse trough at the far end of the deserted Main Street.

'You can see the old mine-workin's up ahead, Capt'n,' the miner said. 'The four fellas you're after are diggin' on the west face.' He gave a gap-toothed grin. 'They won't know you're here until they're gazin' at the barrels of your boys' guns.'

He was riding between the one-eyed captain and his stone-faced sergeant. Behind them in a double file were sixteen of the toughest looking, armed-up men he had ever seen. Knocking the edge of his well-being thoughts that for fingering the ex-raiders the captain was handing him more money than he could earn hacking out of the ground in six months was the grim realization that if the red-leg captain thought that he was playing them false the sergeant would shoot him dead in the bat of an eye.

As if reading his thoughts he heard the captain call out, 'Ride alert, men!' Then came the squeaking of leather as rifles were drawn out of their boots.

The captain was taking no chances. If one thing he had bloodily learned during the war it was the certain fact that cornered reb guerillas fought back as vicious as

36

a pack of boxed-in wolves. Even if there were only four of them up ahead in an ambushcade situation they could inflict serious casualties on his small command.

The sudden attack came in the shape of one single bullet that rattled through the timber like a cannon shot, scattering the column and blowing away the back of the miner's head in a mess of bloody pieces, hurtling him out of his saddle.

As he was remounting, Luther heard the sound of the single shot. By its deep resounding boom it could have only been fired from the heavy gun the sharpshooter, Jake, had been holding. He waited a moment or two but heard no more gunfire. The lone shot, he would bet his life on it, had heralded the death of the informer. Luther smiled. It sounded as though that business Lucius had spoken of had been settled. He heeled his horse's ribs; it was time he got himself well clear of Willow Creek. It wouldn't be long before a one-eyed Union officer showed up, as mad as hell at not capturing four of Colonel Mosby's boys. He would be wondering who it was who had warned the guerillas of his coming and red legs tended to be heavy-handed in their dealings with folk they suspected of still favouring the old Southern cause.

'Do you want me to send four of the men up into those trees, Capt'n, to flush out the bastards?' Sergeant Parker asked.

The troop were sheltering behind their horses, rifles at the ready, resting across their saddles as they eagle-eyed the timber-covered slope.

Captain Chartris shook his head and sheathed his pistol. 'They'll be long gone by now, Sergeant,' he replied. He looked down at the dead miner. 'They've done what they wanted to do. Whoever killed him did so from those rocks above the tree-line, giving himself plenty of time to cut and run for it before we could get up there. A single-shot, long-range rifle fired by a sharp-shooter. If they wanted to make a fight of it they would have laid an ambush at the beginning of those trees and opened fire on us with repeating rifles.' The captain's face twisted in the briefest of smiles. 'And it is quite possible that I wouldn't be having this conversation with you, Sergeant.' Then his face steeled over again. 'Troopers Burke and Shelley, bury the body! We'll carry on to the mine, Sergeant, with the rest of the detail and try and find out from the other miners where the rebs are heading for. And just as importantly, who warned them that we were coming.'

After questioning the dozen or so miners still work-ing on the hillside all the captain discovered was that a rider had come up to the mine and had spoken to the missing men no more than an half an hour before they showed up. A rider, that was all. No description of him or his horse. Which didn't surprise the captain any. He hadn't expected any more intelligence. He was well aware that there were a lot of reb sympathizers in the Nations. The man who had told him where the former reb guerilla fighters were had been a lucky break, though not so lucky for him.

'We'll ride back to the Lodge Pole camp, Sergeant,' he said. 'Spend a few days there to allow the men to check on their gear and rest the horses before we go out on patrol again.'

FIVE

One hour's ride out of Willow Creek Luther saw the
thin wavery wisp of camp-fire smoke and wondered if
he was going to meet up with another bunch of ex-reb
guerilla fighters. His highly tuned warning nerves
twanged, stopping him from riding straight on into the
camp. Instead he knee'd his horse down into a dry wash
running in the direction of the smoke. When he was
close enough to the camp to smell the burning kindling
he dismounted and climbed up the sandy bank and
peered over the rim of the wash at the camp, a mere
thirty feet away. He saw three men, two squatting at the
fire, the third, a much older man, sitting roped to a
tree, the sunlight winking off the lawman's badge
pinned to his coat.

Luther gave out a low, soft whistle of surprise. Since
leaving Texas all he had been doing was coming across
troubled men at camp-fires and the old marshal was
definitely in trouble. How to get him out of that situation made Luther think hard for a few moments. He
took a longer look at the marshal's captors. Then he
grinned. He would come on the pair Colonel Mosby

style. Although they had the hard-faced looks of up and coming *pistoleros* they were still young enough to be panicked into making a bolt for it when he rode down on them, shouting and a'hollering and blazing away with both pistols. He slid down the wash and got back on to his saddle and rode further along the wash to get ahead of the camp.

A cursing Marshal Harper tugged ineffectively at the ropes binding him to the tree. He didn't think he was getting too old to be one of Judge Isaac Parker's marshals, he damn well *knew* he was too old, letting the Jackson cousins, two backwoods, hillbilly killers to sneak up on him. The cousins were barely out of their teens, but had built up a rep of killings and robberies of owlhoots twice their age. The marshal had never attempted to administer the law this far west in the Nations but had turned down a backup partner. Now that foolishness was about to get him dead, after the cousins had finished eating the meal he had prepared for himself.

They wouldn't shoot him, they could have done that when they first jumped him; instead one of them had bent his pistol over his head that left him with one almighty headache when he came to, to find he was trussed up to a tree. The sons-of-bitches would make his passing over look like an accident, not wanting to bring extra trouble on their heads by gunning down one of Judge Parker's lawmen. The pair would be well aware that the judge would set his full-blood Indian trackers on their trail, sign readers who would follow their tracks as long as it took to catch up with them. Then if still alive they would be hauled back to Fort Smith to swing

40

by the neck on the six-rope scaffold outside Judge Parker's law court. All the marshal could hope, to escape his fate, was that the cousins would get careless and give him the chance to get the upper hand. And that, the marshal thought gloomily, would take one hell of a miracle and he couldn't see a such-like event being granted by the Almighty to an old sinner like himself.

Luther, howling the rebel yell, came out of the shelter of a small stand of timber to cover the distance to the camp at a mad-ass gallop. He had the reins wrapped loosely over his left wrist allowing him to have a cocked pistol in both hands. He clung to his saddle by the seat of his pants and tightness of his knees pressing into its flanks.

The two men at the fire leapt to their feet and Luther saw their alarmed looks as they spun round to face him. He fired two loads from each pistol close by their heads to give the impression he meant business and to send them running scared for their mounts. They surprised him by holding their ground and grabbing for their guns. He swore. It was for real now or he would get himself dead.

Luther fired as fast as he could thumb back the hammers. The cousins folded at the knees under the deadly hail and slipped sideways to the ground, their pistols unfired. Then his high stepping horse was on top of them, and its iron-shod hoofs stamped out what dying flicker of life was left in their bodies. Luther calmed his horse and dismounted, trembling slightly at the unexpected turn of events. He was leaving a trail of death behind him, he thought grimly. He heard the tied-up lawman call out, 'Have no feelin's of regrets,

41

friend! Those two sonsuvbitches were long due for plantin' and you've saved me from an early grave. They could have cut and run for it but they chose the hard way and lost.' Luther walked across to the lawman drawing his knife.

Luther and Marshal Harper were sitting at the fire drinking coffee while the old lawman was recovering from his pistol-whipping; Luther had bathed the caked blood from the marshal's wound. Behind them were two piles of stones covering the bodies of the cousins. They had exchanged names and Luther was relating the reason why he had left Texas and how he had been forced to shoot the two bounty-hunters. He didn't mention his warning the miners, or his decision to wage a one-man war against the red legs. The old man was a US marshal and he could take unkindly to actions that he could reckon were law breaking.

'Now I've heard that there's a bunch of red legs hereabouts seeking out men who once rode with 'Bloody' Bill and Quantrill,' he finished. Luther opined that he had said enough to convince the marshal that he was a man who had to keep on the move to save his neck.

The marshal drew on his pipe a couple of times before saying, 'Yeah, I've seen those red legs you spoke of on the trail, though not close enough to pass the time of day with.' He shot Luther a questioning glance. 'Are they on your trail, Luther?'

'Not yet,' Luther replied. 'But if I bump into them on some lonely spot and they find out I'm a Texan, an ex-reb, why they could string me up just for the hell of it. I don't know where those stone-faced sonsuvbitches are, Marshal, so it means that I've got a crick in my neck looking which way and every way in case they jump me.'

Marshal Harper took another few sucks at his pipe. 'As an Abe Lincoln man,' he said 'I don't hold any bad feelings against you rebs; a man does what he feels comfortable doin', and furthermore you saved my hide so it's up to me to try and help you out. I think I've come up with a plan that oughta ease the pain in your neck somewhat.' He grinned at Luther's puzzled look.

'I'll swear you in as a temporary deputy marshal,' he continued. 'I'll fix you up with a tin star to make it legal like.' He reached into his coat pocket and pulled out a sheaf of dog-eared papers. Giving them a quick look, he peeled one off and handed it to Luther. 'That's a warrant for the arrest of one Whitney Purcell, also known as "Snake". A part Nigra, part Injun bad-ass, wanted for several counts of murder and stealin'. 'Course you you don't have to seek out Snake, but it means you can make yourself known to the sheriffs in what passes for townships in this section of the Nations as a state marshal and be able to ask them if the red legs have passed through their towns without seemin' to be a nosy stranger. And no red leg would dare even look fish-eyed at one of Judge Parker's lawmen. Why, the old firebrand himself would come ass-kickin' out here if he got word that an upstart Yankee captain was harassin' one of his men.'

Luther grinned and without any hesitation he said, 'I'll take that badge, Marshal Harper; start swearing me in. Keeping on the look-out for this owlhoot, Snake, will keep me occupied till I get the feeling it's OK for me to ride back down to Texas.'

They both got to their feet, the marshal smiling. 'My ugly mug is well known hereabouts,' he said. 'So you can have my badge.' He unclipped the badge on his vest and pinned it on Luther's shirt. 'We'll dispense with the rigmarole of swearin' in, Luther, only old man Parker's legalized to do that.' He handed Luther a crumpled wad of paper dollars. 'That oughta tide you and your horse over grubwise for a week or so.' He saw Luther's look of rejection. 'Take it; it's legal expenses. You're entitled to money to buy reloads, but I see you ain't short of shells, Marshal.'

As Luther mounted up to ride out, Marshal Harper felt it was only right and proper to warn the new peace officer that along with the protection the badge gave him against the red legs it could also make him a likely target for any desperado roaming about the territory who had a natural hatred against all badge-wearing men unless he kept his head low until he drifted back south again. But Luther Kane had proved to him that he wasn't a man who rode around dangerous situations.

'Now you take care, Marshal,' he said. 'Seein' a marshal's badge kinda riles some of the hard men in the territory, makes them reach for their pistols.'

'I'll be OK,' Luther replied. 'I'll tread carefully.' Though he reasoned that it was better odds for him to stay alive meeting up with Snake, or any other lawbreaker than risk a head-on clash with a band of reb-hating red legs. Making sure that his badge was showing, he tugged gently at the reins and his horse stepped out smartly. He turned in his saddle and raised his hand to Marshal Harper before the trail dropped down behind a small ridge.

Marshal Harper thought that Luther Kane, who had come through one hell of a war, shouldn't have to ride all armed up to meet trouble the war should have seen ended. He should have been allowed to tend to his boss's cows in peace.

SIX

Jethro Lawson, working on his bottom land that ran along the Lodge Pole river, eased the reins of the plough horse from his aching shoulders. He loosened the rag around his neck and wiped the sweat off his face, and saw the line of riders moving along the river ridge away to his right. Blurred and shimmering in the noon-day heat, they had the appearance of what the Indians called ghost riders. Jethro cursed. There was no mistaking who they were. The one-eyed captain and his murderous scum were back along the Lodge Pole. And the sons-of-bitches were riding in a double column as though they were regular horse soldiers.

Had the captain sniffed him out that he had once given food and grain to reb brush boys? Jethro didn't think so, or the red legs would have poured down from the high ground and strung him up on the big old oak by the water's edge there. Then they would have put a torch to his home and barn in front of Cassie, his wife, and Betty Anne, his daughter.

Though he had fought for the Union as a rifleman he'd had no regrets helping out men who had once been his enemies. The war was over for the soldiers on both sides and yet some ex-rebs were being hunted down like wild and dangerous animals. Slowly and painfully the country was getting back to being a single nation again, and the brutal actions of the red legs weren't helping that process.

Jethro watched the red-leg detail ride out of sight. He had only ploughed half his field but the sighting of the red legs had knocked all the edge he'd had for ploughing out of him. He unhitched the horse from the plough and led it back to the barn.

Jethro was even more upset when he walked into his shack. Two men, as gaunt-faced and ragged-assed as any saddle tramps he had seen were sitting at his table eating his food with the speed of men who hadn't eaten for a long spell. A third stranger, with a dirty, blood-stained bandage of sorts was lying back in his favourite chair being spoon fed by Betty Anne. Jethro's face became as tight-skinned-looking as his unexpected and definitely unwelcome guests.

Panic stricken, he stepped back to the door and cast out a nervous glance, half expecting to see the red-leg patrol pulling up outside his front porch. Jethro had heard of how the Blackfeet, instead of hunting their game the normal way by tracking them, just set alight to sections of the woods or prairie to drive the game out into the open. The blasted red legs, he thought angrily, didn't need to light any fires to flush out their game, their very presence set the dozens of ex-rebs in the territory scattering for safer spots to hole-up in. Like his home.

But what the hell could he do, Jethro reasoned?

Order them to get out of his house, pronto? The two wolfing at the table could maybe stand another three, four cold-night camps, but the reb in his chair looked all in. Asking him to go would be like signing his death warrant. He gave the trio of trouble a sickly welcoming grin.

Both of the men at the table got to their feet. One of them said, 'We're mighty grateful for what your women-folk have done for us, friend. We know we could bring big trouble on you, so as soon as we've eaten we'll ride out.'

Before Jethro could reply his wife butted in. 'Nonsense!' she said firmly. 'Your friend there is in no fit state to sit up on a horse, let alone ride it! There's a cave in the hillside well back from the house which used to be our root cellar, I'll fix it up for you all, blankets, oil stove, comfortable enough to spend several days there. You'll be OK there. I know the red legs have a camp just along the Lodge Pole, but they haven't bothered us any. Isn't that so, Jethro?'

'Yeah,' replied Jethro, not telling his wife that the red legs were back in their camp. If the bastards were across the line in Kansas they would be too damn close for his peace of mind. But he knew he was wasting his breath arguing with his wife, she had decided that the rebs could stay and that was that.

'I'll gather up some blankets and dig out that old stove,' he said, with more cheer in his voice than he was feeling. 'Now you boys get sat down and eat your fill, Ma don't like any of her food being left on the plates. I take it that your mounts are hidden in that stand of timber at the back of the house.' Jethro got an acknowledging nod from the reb spokesman. 'I'll unsaddle them and take all your gear to the cellar; the horses I'll put in with the rest of the farm stock.' He gave them a nod and strode out of the shack to do the chores, and worry himself to an early grave in private.

SEVEN

Luther had just cleared a lopsided signpost that read
Lodge Pole Bend, Pop. 40, then he saw a line of buildings on either side of a dirt street and thought it advis-
able to buy extra rations and grain for his horse. He
had several days of tracking ahead of him to pick up the
red-legs trail and he had no idea if he would ride into
another town. Riding in closer, Luther could see what
he thought must be most of the male citizens of the
town bunched around an adobe built building at the
far end of the street.

Curious to the reason that had brought the men out
on to the street, he rode past the general store until he
could hear the mob's angry shouts and notice that the
building was the sheriff's office and jailhouse. He drew
up his mount at the edge of the protesters, still unno-
ticed by any of them.

An anxious-faced, beer-gutted man wearing a
lawman's badge, was standing on the porch trying to
reason with the shouting men. He was flanked by what
Luther took to be two of his deputies, holding shotguns
across their chests, and looking as pinch-assed-faced as
the sheriff.

'We've come for that murderin' no-good Nigra, Sheriff!' a man at the front of the crowd yelled. 'We're aimin' to have the sonuvabitch dance on air from the feed barn's hoist for the killin' of Luke Slade!'

'There'll be no lynchin' in my town, Meaker!' the sheriff replied defiantly, his hand dropping on to his belted pistol. 'So you fellas get back to work before Meaker's rantin' lands you all in big trouble! Johnson is stayin' behind bars until Marshal Harper makes his call here and takes him across to Fort Smith where Judge Parker will decide whether he hangs or not! And you boys oughta know before you take the law into your own hands that Johnson claims that he shot Slade when he found him rapin' his fourteen-year-old granddaughter!'

'So the sonuvabitch claims!' Meaker snarled out. 'All we know is that a Nigra shot dead a white man which is a hangin' matter in a white-man's town! If you don't hand him over we'll stomp over you and your deputies and take him!'

Meaker's tirade had the mob's blood running wild and they pressed closer to the porch forcing the sheriff and his deputies to step back involuntarily to the office walls.

Luther had lived through many a wartime hairy situation and knew how some men would act in such-like situations. He knew for a fact that if the loud-mouthed spokesman of the lynch mob pushed it to a showdown the two deputies would chicken out, not use their riot guns on men who must be their drinking buddies. The sheriff would be on his own and by his fear-frozen look he knew it. He was accepting being a loser in his own town either way. The mob could rush him and take his prisoner, maybe killing him in the process, or they could heed his warning and vote him out of office at the next election, though in spite of the hopelessness of his position he was still enough of a lawman to risk all to protect his prisoner. Luther, wearing the badge of one of Judge Parker's marshals, thought it was time he backed up a fellow lawman's stand.

He drew out a pistol and fired a single shot. The shell tore splinters from a porch post close by the mob leader's head causing him to spring back in alarm and stemmed the mob's baying for blood. The would-be lynchers spun round and faced him with scowled fixed looks. Luther fish-eyed them back, with pistols held now in both hands, the right gun held directly at the leading agitator.

In the belief that a mob is only as strong as its leader Luther opined that if he could force the hot-headed Mr Meaker to back down the rest of the blood seekers would walk away. He truly hoped so, or he would be making his first arrest as a state marshal by arresting himself for gunning down several male citizens of Lodge Pole Bend. He drew back the hammers of the Colts, hoping the mob could hear their blood-chilling clicks. Bluffing time was here.

'As the sheriff said, go about your business,' he said conversationally. 'Leave the carrying out of the law to the lawmen, or I'll apt to be forced to shed some blood and being a US marshal, Judge Parker has given me the right to do that if I reckon that the peace of a community is in jeopardy. And this assembly is in no way peaceful.'

Luther's hawk-eyed gaze swept over the men, watching for twitching hands sneaking towards pistols.

Though Meaker's face was still twisted in anger he was doing some rapid-fire thinking as he eyed the pistol pointing straight at him. Was the big stone-faced son-of-a bitch bluffing, he asked himself? He didn't think so; Judge Parker's bloodhounds weren't noted for making statements and not backing them up with guns. Meaker risked a quick glance over his shoulder, the sheriff had thrown down on him as well. Then he knew for certain he would be the first man shot if he still wanted the hanging to go ahead. He licked fear-dried lips and tried to keep that fear from showing in his face.

'OK, boys,' he managed to croak. 'Let's get off the street. We don't want that Nigra to be responsible for any more white men's deaths.' With a final drop-dead glare at Luther he walked away from the jailhouse towards the bar across the street. The rest of the mob peeled off, some following Meaker into the bar.

Luther sheathed his right-hand pistol, the other gun he thrust down the top of his pants. He drew his rifle from its boot, levered a shell into the chamber and switched his gaze over on to the door of the bar. He had made a hot-head eat crow in front of his neighbours and it was not only Indians who take badly losing face badly. Only when he judged that Meaker was not about to come fire-balling out of the bar with his pistol blazing did he swing down from his saddle and, with his rifle still held ready to bring up into action, he walked across to the sheriff and his deputies.

The sheriff, all smiles, stepped down from his stoop and shook Luther's hand with all the genuine fervour of a man knowing he had escaped a gun fight he knew he would have lost.

'Marshal,' he said. 'That bastard, Meaker had me and my deputies pinned down well and truly between a rock and a hard place. He would have gunned us down for sure if you hadn't showed up. I'm Sheriff Preston, if Judge Parker ain't mentioned me to you. It's usually Marshal Harper who makes the trip to Lodge Pole Bend to see if I'm holdin any man he's got papers on in my jail. The old goat ain't got himself bushwhacked, has he?'

Luther grinned, 'No, he's still riding around, least-ways he was a couple of days back when he swore me in as deputy marshal. He's allowing me to work on my own to kinda familiarize myself with the territory. Luther Kane is my name.'

Sheriff Preston turned and spoke to his deputies. 'See to Marshal Kane's horse, Bob. Jimmy, stay put on the porch and keep a watchful eye on the bar door. Meaker is a mean, unforgivin' bastard, Marshal; he could get those fellas in there with him roused up in lynchin' mood again with the rattlesnake juice they serve across the bar as whiskey. The sooner you can haul old Johnson off to Fort Smith the sooner Lodge Pole Bend will quieten down. I could have taken Johnson over to Newton, the nearest town, but once the law-abidin' citizens there got wind of a killer in their jail the sheriff there would have the same necktie party trouble as I've had. Come inside and we'll talk it over.'

Being a US marshal, albeit a temporary one, Luther thought, as he stepped into the sheriff's office was anything but a quiet life. He had tangled with a lynch mob, and now had to take charge of a man accused of murder. Not forgetting the possibility that he could tangle with the bad-ass 'breed, Snake Whitney.

'It's OK, Johnson,' the sheriff said to his prisoner sitting on the cot in the only cell in the jailhouse. 'A US marshal is here to escort you to Judge Parker's courthouse at Fort Smith. He's also forced Meaker to back down; you ain't about to be lynched.'

Luther glanced into the cell at the prisoner, an elderly white-haired sorry-looking man. He didn't have the cut of a killer, though by what he had heard the sheriff say he had knifed a white man to death. If he did decide to escort Johnson to Fort Smith it would mean that he couldn't keep a watch on the red legs and what next fugitive bunch of ex-brush boys they were setting out to hunt down. And somehow it didn't seem right to hand over the old man to Judge Parker so he could string him up on his gallows for doing a deed any man, black, red, brown or white, would do, fight to save his close kin from coming to harm. He knew that the Judge wouldn't see it that way: he'd hung men for thieving. The old man was escaping a lynching so he could be legally hanged.

'I'd advise you to get Johnson outa town right now, Marshal,' the sheriff said, 'while the bastards are still bellied up to the bar. I can fix you up with a horse for Johnson and some extra rations.' He cast Luther a pleading glance. 'That's if you ain't in hot pursuit of any wrongdoer.'

Luther could understand the sheriff's haste to get the man out of his town. A lynch mob is trouble a lawman doesn't want to face twice in a day.

'I'm carrying a warrant for the arrest of a Mr Whitney,' he replied. 'But I'm not choking in his trail dust. And I've no idea where he's hiding out.'

The sheriff laughed, the first laugh of the day. 'Snake Whitney! Why that thievin' sonuvabitch must be in Kansas, m'be Missouri by now. Two days ago him and another no-good asshole tried to rob the bank at Younger's Creek, a town north of here. But the raid didn't turn out as Snake planned. Half the citizens of the town lined up on Main Street with their Winchesters and cut loose at the pair as they came runnin' out of the bank, shootin' Snake's pard well and truly dead. The last they saw of him was one helluva dust cloud raised by his horse headin' for the Kansas border.'

'It seems that Snake Whitney is out of Judge Parker's jurisdiction now, Sheriff,' Luther said. He looked in on Johnson again. 'So I can take that prisoner to Fort Smith.'

Which Luther had no intention of doing. He had come to a firm decision. Saving some ex-rebs from the lynch-mob law the red legs dished out was more important than giving Judge Parker the pleasure of hanging an old man who shouldn't be in jail at all.

Once he was clear of Lodge Pole Bend he would give Johnson the chance to make a run for it. By the time Sheriff Preston found out that his prisoner hadn't made it to Fort Smith and began to wonder what had happened to him and the old man, he ought to be back in Texas as straw boss of the T Star once more.

Sheriff Preston, much relieved at getting a load of trouble off his hands, felt like doing a jig. Eagerly he

56

said, 'I'll get that horse and the extra rations, Marshal. You can sneak Johnson out by the back way. You'll be well along the trail eastwards before Meaker realizes he ain't got anyone to hang.'

That was wishful thinking on the sheriff's part; Meaker was still determined to have his hanging. Gut-chewing angry at his failure to carry out a lynching he wasn't drowning his disappointment with rotgut whiskey, he was standing at the bar scowling at the jail-house and silently dirty-mouthing the US marshal who had scotched his plans. And thinking hard of how he could still put his rope round Johnson's neck. His scowl changed to a puzzled look as he saw one of the deputies hurry along the street and go into the general store, then come out holding two well-filled gunny sacks. Then the deputy cut down the side alley that led to the livery barn. Ten minutes or so later, the deputy came out on to the street, rein leading a saddled-up horse with the sacks slung across its back. Meaker bared his teeth in a merci-less grin. He was no longer puzzled: the son-of-a-bitch marshal was about to sneak Johnson out of town.

Meaker looked at the would-be lynchers drinking at the bar, men he once had a rep with as a tough *hombre*, a man other men stepped aside for. That fear of him was gone, though none of them had told him so to his face. Meaker's fierce grin showed again. He reckoned he knew just how he could walk tall among them again. The boys would get their promised necktie party after all.

At the rear of the jailhouse Luther was saying his farewells to the sheriff. He and his prisoner were in their saddles.

'You're sure you don't want Johnson's hands shackled, Marshal?' Sheriff Preston asked. 'It's a long tiring haul to Fort Smith.'

Luther looked at his prisoner, as broken spirited as he had been in his cell. He thin-smiled. 'You're not aiming to cause me any trouble on the trail, are you, boy?'

Being called a boy by someone half his age was something Lemuel Johnson accepted, especially from a man he guessed was a Texan. He hadn't been foolish enough to think that the war, fought to free his race from slavery, meant that he could now walk as an equal alongside the whites. Yet he had to admit that two white men had saved him from a lynching, though that didn't mean he had escaped being hanged; it had only delayed his ultimate fate. But, as the sheriff had just stated to the marshal, it was long ways to Fort Smith. For a fleeting moment or two Lemuel lost his haunted look as he felt the hard comforting pressure of the knife stuck down his right boot. When the chance came he would make it a whole heap longer for the white-man's law to get him to Fort Smith to stand trial for killing an animal. He had been determined to use the knife on himself rather than let the white trash have the pleasure of hanging him. Downcast-eyed he said, 'You'll get no trouble from me, boss.'

'Good,' replied Luther. 'Let's ride then.'

When the first dip in the trail cut them out of sight of Lodge Pole Bend Luther thought it was time to tell Johnson he was no longer his prisoner. He pulled up his mount, Lemuel stopped alongside him wondering if the Texan had decided to to bind his hands after all, which would make it all that much more difficult to get at his knife and use it with good effect.

'Mr Johnson,' Luther began, 'for reasons I'm not going to explain you are no longer in my custody. So my advice is to get to hell out this section of the territory, pronto. Kansas, m'be, where Judge Parker don't hold sway. I'm giving you your freedom now reckoning that you must live close by and you might want to pick up what bits and pieces you can carry. You won't be able to keep the horse; someone could recognize its brand and ask you some awkward questions.' Luther cold-smiled. 'I figure you've had your bellyful of awkward-minded white men. Mr Johnson.'

Lemuel sat still and silent in his saddle, giving Luther a long apprehensive look.

Luther's grin had warmth in it this time. 'I'm not about to shoot you in the back, Mr Johnson, for trying to "escape"; I'm not a back shooter. Yes, I fought for the South but I did so for my State, Texas, not to uphold slavery. You're free to go, but as I said, don't hang about too long this close to Lodge Pole Bend or you'll put me in one helluva predicament that could see me put behind bars for not carrying out my duty.'

Lemuel kept his searching gaze on Luther for a few more seconds more before finally saying, 'I believe you, Marshal. But just to get things straight, that white trash, Slade, did rape my granddaughter and I ain't got any regrets killing him. Her mother, my daughter-in-law, took her north to Kansas where she has some close kin. Her husband, my only boy, was killed at Fort Wagner fighting for the Union. I'll join them there. What gear I've got at my shack can be slung on the back of my old mule.' Lemuel favoured Luther with a ghost of a smile.

'You don't have to tell me it's not wise for me to stay long in these parts, Marshal.'

Meaker came slowly, on foot, through the brush, rifle held ready. The marshal and his prisoner pulling up their mounts to talk made it easy for him to get the drop on the lawman. Meaker had a burning urge to hang Johnson but he shied away from shooting dead one of Judge Parker's marshals to get his hands on the man, or he would meet the same fate he had in mind for Johnson. All what was needed was to put the marshal out of action until Johnson had finished dancing on air.

Then he would be quite happy to weather what trouble the marshal would raise. Meaker didn't think it would amount to much. After all who would lose sweat over the hanging of a Negro murderer? He was only saving the law the expense of an official hangman.

'You just sit tight, Marshal,' he said, as he stepped out on to the trail. 'I ain't lookin' for trouble but if you get in my way I'll wing you for sure.' He glared at Lemuel with a snarl of a grin. 'Now you just step down, boy, you're kinda overdue for a hangin'.'

Luther twisted ass and faced Meaker, rapidly working out his options. Like should he do as Meaker said, or could he yank out his belly-hugging pistol and pull off a shot before the ambusher blew him out of his saddle. His Texas pride favoured the second option, come what may. His prisoner saying, 'Don't get yourself shot for me, Marshal,' stayed his wild-ass move. He cursed. The old man was right: Meaker held all the high cards.

He watched Johnson dismount and walk across to Meaker, Meaker keeping his eyes and rifle on him.

Johnson seemed to stumble just in front of Meaker then quickly regained his balance. To his surprise he saw that Meaker seemed to lose his footing and stagger backwards a pace or two before falling, rifle dropping out of widespread arms, hitting the ground heavily, to lie there unmoving. Only then did Luther catch the glint of a knife stuck in Meaker's chest. He let out his breath in a long hiss. He had never seen a slicker killing.

Johnson walked back to him, expressionless. 'You can take me to Fort Smith, Marshal,' he said, voice as flat-toned as his face. 'But they can't hang me twice.'

It was several moments before Luther spoke. Another series of life and death options were flashing before his eyes. This time only Johnson's life was at stake.

'Mr Johnson,' he finally said. 'I gave you your freedom and what you did here hasn't changed my mind. Meaker held a rifle on a US marshal; he could have pulled the trigger at not being too happy at me for stopping him lynching you. You probably saved my life. Be on your way, Mr Johnson, I'll sort things out here.'

Lemuel managed a smile, the first for a long time. 'I hope that reason you spoke of, Marshal, the one that's allowin' you to free me, works out in your favour.'

'I hope so, Mr Johnson, I truly hope so,' Luther replied soberly. 'And you look out for your kin up there in Kansas.'

Not until the old man had gone from his view did Luther dismount and go across to Meaker's body and begin to 'sort' things out. He pulled the knife out of Meaker's chest and threw it far away. Grabbing hold of

the rifle, he fired three loads into the air then still holding the weapon lifted Meaker's body on to his shoulder
and carried it across to the brush on the side of the
trail. There he let it and the rifle drop to the ground.
He drew one of his pistols and fired a single shot into
the knife wound. Then he stood back to contemplate
the situation he had created. A failed bushwhacking
that had got Meaker dead, or so Luther hoped when
Meaker's body was discovered.

Sheriff Preston would work out that things had
happened the way he could see them. Meaker, mad at
the marshal for making him back down, had tried to
ambush him on the trail and take his prisoner. Luther,
knowing that Meaker had boxed the sheriff into one
hell of a tight corner, didn't think that the lawman
would investigate the shooting any further. As far as he
was concerned the marshal and his prisoner were well
along the trail to Fort Smith, unharmed.

Luther gave a satisfied grunt at an awkward situation
being resolved, though somewhat tempered with the
disappointment that he had fogotten to ask the sheriff
if the red legs had passed through his town. Though,
thinking logically, the one-eyed captain wouldn't stay
long in Willow Creek; he would be keen to get his
manhunters back on the trail again to carry on with his
blood-crazy mission, that of tracking down ex-reb
guerillas and see them hang.

Luther could see the Lodge Pole river snaking and
looping its way eastwards across the flats, so banking on
the red legs moving northwards, and having to ford the
river, it should be an easy scout to pick up the sign of
fifteen or so horses being ridden in a column. Then

came the big problem, how was he going to find out where any ex-marauders were holed-up and warn them of their danger? He could only play it as it came and prayed that luck rode with him. But, first things first, Luther thought optimistically, like finding where his enemy was. Although there were several hours of good tracking light left he decided to make camp, wanting the red-leg column to get well ahead of him, not wishing to show his presence to them unless forced to do so. Then he could face them with all the authority of a state marshal.

Marshal Harper was having grave doubts about his wisdom of giving Luther Kane a marshal's badge. It was supposed to have given the Texan protection against possible harassment by the red legs. It had turned out not to have been one of his better ideas after hearing Sheriff Preston's account of how the new marshal had faced down a howling lynch mob and then had to shoot his way out of an ambush, killing his ambusher.

Marshal Harper had swung east to Lodge Pole Bend after checking that the sheriff at Palmer's Flats wasn't holding any lawbreakers in his jailhouse he'd had papers on, and on the off chance that Marshal Kane had passed through the town. Ever since Luther had left he'd had nagging doubts that by giving him a lawman's badge he was putting him into more danger than he already was. Now, by what he had heard, he had no doubts that he had done just that. The Texan, lawman or not, was a man who seemed to attract trouble, three-dead-men kind of trouble, though none of it was of his own making. And the marshal thanked his

Maker that Luther had got out of his latest brush with trouble safely.

'He and his prisoner must be well on the way to Fort Smith by now, marshal,' he heard Sheriff Preston say.

'Yeah, yeah, I reckon so,' he replied, his mind still unsettled about the wellbeing of the man, who with the best intentions, he had made a marshal. Leastways, he thought, the closer Luther got to Fort Smith the least chance he had of meeting up with trouble again. It was a burden off his mind, now he could get down to some law enforcing of his own, and make sure *he* didn't ride into trouble. After saying his goodbyes to Sheriff Preston he mounted up and rode out of Lodge Pole Bend by the north trail.

EIGHT

Whitney 'Snake' Purcell, panting and sweating as heavily as a blown horse, was thinking he was in one hell of a fix. He was crawling on his belly through a close grown belt of thickets and cane that was tearing at his clothes and raising deep blood oozing scratches on his hands and face, hoping to give his pursuers the slip, a bunch of red legs up on horses who could spot any unusual movements in the undergrowth and close in on it, guns firing.

Snake was wishing now he had really quit the Nations and crossed over into Kansas after the failed bank raid. It was the first time he had worked with a partner and he had left him lying in the dust outside the bank all shot to hell. He had ridden north, almost to the border, making sure that he had been seen and recognized by the occasional sodbuster working on his land, eyewitnesses to prove that Snake Purcell was Kansas bound. Just before the Kansas line, opining that he had fooled the lawmen that he was leaving their territory, he swung south planning to carry on with his thieving before those who had an interest in capturing him caught on to the surprising fact that Snake was back in business in the Nations. Then his stupid horse had to break its front leg stepping into a gopher hole and he'd had to shoot it. Without a horse, he thought angrily, how the hell could he rob a stage?

He had set off walking until he could see the Lodge Pole river army post ahead and sat down to weigh up the risks of lifting a horse from an army post, or keep on walking until he could steal one from a ranch or a farm. Reckoning that the longer he was without a mount the more likely he was of being picked up by the law, risky or not, the taking an army horse was the better option.

Snake made a quick circuit of the stockade, noting with a grin that the sentry at the big double gates was dozing with his back up against one of them and that the horse line was only a few yards from the rear wall of the post. Snake's grin widened. The blue belly would soon come alive when he galloped past him clinging low down on its flanks in his Indian relations' style.

Snake took a last look through the stockade planking and could see no signs of movement in the compound other than the idle swishing of the horses' tails flicking away the flies. The post garrison must have their heads down in the big hut until it was cool enough for them to do their chores. Snake's confident smile stretched to his ears. He had as good as got himself a mount.

Snake used his knife to prise apart two of the planks at the rear of the stockade, wide enough for him to squeeze through. He was practically within touching distance of the horse he had picked out, when a soldier suddenly stepped out of a small hut right in front of him and began to slip his suspenders back over his shoulders. Then he caught sight of Snake and clawed for his belted pistol. Snake's confident feelings vanished in a flash.

He whirled round and hared back to the opening in the fence and hurled himself through it as shells thunked into the planking either side of him. What gave more speed to his flight was that he had seen that the man who had come out of the crapper wore red leather boots, red-leg's boots – lynching men. Snake sobbed. He had stirred up a pack of starving wolves. As he made it to the edge of the wasteland he cast a wild look over his shoulder and saw five, six horsemen come pounding out of the post. The hunt for him was on in earnest. Then it was down on his belly, eating dirt, zig-zagging this way and that way until he had lost all sense of direction. His rifle hindering his progress so much that he discarded it.

The ground beneath Snake began to dampen and soon he was ploughing his way through several inches of water; he had reached the edge of the Lodge Pole. Once it was deep enough to swim in he would be able to move faster and if he kept close to the thick reeds running along the river's edge he should be able to elude his red-leg hunters. Snake stood up to risk a look around him. Through sweat glazed eyes he saw that his pursuers were only hazy figures riding bunched up well behind him. The bastards couldn't find his trail. He slipped into deeper water and started to swim downstream, every stroke taking him further away from a hanging.

Luther had picked up the trail of the red leg column and felt that he was getting back into the war again. He had stepped down from his horse to tighten up a saddle strap when he heard a slight rustling sound behind him. He let go of the buckle and both of his hands reached under his wide-tailed duster. He heard the scuffling noise again, nearer this time. And had no doubts that someone was trying to creep up on him, some one who hadn't a gun, or he would have called for him to raise his hands, or have shot him dead by now. He made to put a foot in the stirrups but spun round instead, both pistols drawn, hammers thumbed back to eyeball a dripping wet boy hardly out of his teens, and holding a big bladed knife in his right hand.

'Boy,' Luther grated, 'you just drop that blade to the ground or so help me I'll gun you down for the back-stabbing sonuvabitch you are!'

Snake did some eye-balling of his own, at the two pistols trained unwaveringly on him, then at the face of the man holding them. He could see no signs of bluff-ing in the cold-eyed stare. He had definitely lost the edge he thought he'd had over his intended victim. He let go of the knife, silently cursing that if he hadn't lost his pistol in the river things would have been different. He would have had the drop on the po-faced bastard. He was fated, Snake thought, never to get himself a horse. He had a further shock when he caught a glimpse of a marshal's badge on the big man's shirt. 'Shit!' he dirty-mouthed softly; he had exchanged the red-legs' hanging rope for Judge Parker's scaffold at Fort Smith.

Luther took a long assaying look at his would-be attacker: dark skinned, hawk-faced, streaked with blood as though painted for war, and an unwavering stone-eyed gaze. He slow smiled. 'I figure you must be the much sought after Mr Whitney Purcell, or, as it states on the warrant I've got in my pocket, "Snake" Purcell.' And you've presented me with one hell of a problem, boy, he added under his breath.

He'd had no hesitation in giving Mr Johnson his freedom, even if he hadn't let him go for his own reasons, the man was no killer. Snake was a killer, on several counts, and the young bastard tried to kill him. He should carry out his duty as a marshal and take him to Fort Smith. But, by the time he got back from Fort Smith, wearing a badge or not, the red-legs' trail would be cold. His war against them would be over before it had really started.

Before he made up his mind where his duty lay, Luther thought it wise to restrict his prisoner's move-ments by tying him up. Snake might not be showing any feelings in his rattler-eyed gaze but he didn't doubt that the owlhoot's brain would be whirring around figuring of a way to escape his trip to the hangman.

Luther pushed one his pistols back into its sheath, still holding the other one steady on Snake. With the spoken warning that if he so much as blinked an eye he would suffer a painful leg shot, he reached behind him and unhooked his rope from the saddle horn. Then he told Snake to turn round and, coming close up to him, though standing to one side in case Snake back heeled him in the balls, he pressed the pistol muzzle with some force into the nape of Snake's neck, causing him to

69

wince with pain. 'Grasp your hands behind your back, boy, pronto!' he snapped. He quickly slipped the noose around Snake's offered wrists, pulled it tight, giving Snake another pang of pain. Five more twists of the rope and Snake's hands were fully secured.

Luther stepped back and, slipping the pistol into the waistband of his pants, he gave the rope a savage jerk that sent Snake tumbling to the ground like a roped maverick. This time Snake gave out a howl of pain, and a string of curses. Luther dropped down on one knee and in a matter of seconds the rope was round Snake's ankles and he was fully hog tied.

'You sonuvabitch!' Snake cried, eyes blazing with anger. 'You could've busted my arm throwin' me down like that; I ain't some longhorn!'

Luther dragged him on to his feet.

'Do you expect me to shuffle all the way to Fort Smith?' Snake spat out.

'No, I don't,' replied Luther. 'But trussed up like that you're not going to cause me any trouble. And I reckon you can shuffle your way along tied to my saddle until we can reach some place where I can hire a horse for you.' Luther glanced around at the sound of approaching riders. 'M'be one of these gents will be able to tell me where I can get an extra mount.' Luther's nerves tightened on seeing that the three riders were red legs and the leading rider, wearing sergeant's chevrons, was the NCO he had seen in the saloon at Willow Creek. Unconsciously, his right hand hovered above the pistol resting against his belly as he bold-faced them as US Marshal Kane. He felt somewhat easier in his mind as he saw no sign in the big sergeant's face that he remembered seeing him in the saloon.

'So you've caught that sneakin' horse-thief, mister,' Sergeant Barker said. 'That sonuvabitch tried to steal one of our horses back at the post there. We chased him into the wild land alongside the Lodge Pole but he gave us the slip. It looks as though he's been in the river.' Barker gave a wolf's all-tooth snarling grin. 'That'll be the last bath he'll take. We'll take him off your hands, mister, and drag him back to the post; we've a good strong hangin' tree back there!'

Luther drew back his long coat and showed the sergeant his badge. 'Judge Parker at Fort Smith has first call on him, Sergeant,' he said. 'I'm holding a warrant on him.' Then waited, both hands trigger-finger twitching, to see if the sergeant accepted Judge Parker's jurisdiction this far west in the Nations. He had been fretting unnecessarily. The sergeant only gave him a disappointed scowl.

'That's m'be so, Marshal,' he said. 'But it's a long haul to Fort Smith.' He favoured Snake with a sourfaced look. 'That kid looks as though he's got wild Injun blood in him, Marshal. He'll reckon on jumpin' you before you make it to Fort Smith.'

'He could be thinking that way, Sergeant,' replied Luther, giving Snake an equally off-putting look. 'But I figure if I put a shell in his right knee before we set off, the pain that will put his mind off trying to get the better of me!' Luther looked back at the sergeant again. 'It isn't likely he'll be doing a lot of walking about when I get him to Fort Smith.'

Cripple him! Snake swallowed hard, as he felt the taste of bile at the back of his throat. What sort of bloodthirsty bastards was Judge Parker hiring as marshals? His earlier thoughts of as long as he was on his feet he had the chance to outwit his captor were gone.

Sergeant Barker and the two troopers grinned. 'Marshal,' Barker said, 'you're thinkin' like a red leg!'

Luther couldn't understand why he had not handed Snake over to the sergeant. The outlaw was destined to be strung up, why not here? Not making the long trip to Fort Smith would have left him clear to keep tabs on the red-legs' activities. And what he had told Snake about shooting him had been one big bluff to convince the sergeant that his prisoner was in safe hands, though by the sickly look on the kid's face, he believed it. In no way was he going to hand over his prisoner, even a man with the killing rep Snake had, to a red-leg lynching party.

'I haven't got the time to make him walk all the way to Fort Smith, Sergeant.' Luther said. 'So I'll have to see if I can hire a horse hereabouts.'

Sergeant Barker jerked his right thumb over his shoulder. 'There's a homestead five, six miles back along the trail, Marshal, you ought to be able to pick up a horse there.' He gave Luther a parting nod and with one last drop-dead look at Snake pulled his horse's head round. With a curt, 'Let's go, boys!' he dug his heels into his mount's ribs. In a hoof-kicked-up dust cloud the red legs rode back the way they had come.

Luther gazed down at Snake. 'You're not going to make me plug you before I get you a horse, Mr Whitney.'

What 'Mr Whitney' was thinking was that he should

72

have thrown his knife into the son-of-bitch's back, killed him dead. He was already wanted dead or alive; Judge Parker couldn't hang him any higher. Though he didn't show his murderous thoughts outwardly. Po-faced he said, 'I ain't in a position to do anything but gaze at your horse's ass, Marshal.'

Luther grinned. 'Let's go then.' Though he still hadn't worked out what he was going to do with his pris-oner, other than get him a horse, Snake being a bigger burden on foot. Snake felt the tug of the rope and he began to shuffle-step along behind the horse, his pa's Indian blood running hot through him, promising himself that if he ever got the upper hand over the marshal he would lift the bastard's hair for the way he was treating him, like he wasn't human – if he had a knife that is.

Captain Chartris in his office at the outpost's HQ reread the signal from his commanding officer at Fort Lawrence, Kansas. He still couldn't take in what was written there. His command was being disbanded. *Disbanded,* the captain thought angrily. When there were still scores of ex-reb back-shooting brush boys hiding out in the Nations. He had heard hints from the colonel that Washington didn't approve of his rough and ready methods of dealing with ex-rebs. Reconciliation was the government's policy now. Reconciliation be damned, the captain thought vehe-mently. If the army no longer wanted him to hunt down the reb scum he would raise a posse of his own vigi-lantes to do the hunting. He got to his feet and left his office to sound out the now, ex-sergeant Barker on his views about carrying out their campaign against the rebs, and if enough of his former men would be willing to ride with him.

NINE

Luther saw the strips of cleared, cultivated land before he saw the homesteader's shack. They had been on the trail for two hours and he had stopped twice to offer the now dry dust-shrouded Snake a drink. Snake, red rimmed-eyed, refused the water both times. Luther couldn't help but admire the boy's stubborn grit in spite of knowing that he would kill him with the greatest of pleasure if given half a chance.

'We're there, Snake,' he said. 'Let's hope I can get you a mount, as that red-leg sergeant said, it's a long walk to Fort Smith.'

Snake broke his trail silence by dirty-mouthing Luther.

Luther grinned. 'Keep a curb on your tongue, boy. The fella who owns this place could be a Bible-reading man and he won't take kindly hiring out a horse to us if he hears language like that.'

Snake gave him a drop-dead scowl.

Closing in on the shack Luther saw movement just inside the open doors of a barn to his left, and more ominously, the glint of a rifle barrel. Taut-nerved he did some swearing of his own. All he seemed to be doing, he thought bitterly, since he had crossed over into the Nations, was to draw his gun on men who wished him harm. Though if there was Indian trouble in this part of the territory he could understand the need for the homesteader to be on the alert, but in no way could he and Snake be mistaken for a Comanche raiding party.

Then a man came into view round the corner of the shack, also holding a rifle. A third man stepped out of the shack, fisting a pistol and with the whiteness of a bandage showing beneath his open shirt. He was ringed in. For some reason he was the trouble. For a fleeting moment he thought the men must be some of Snake's gang effecting a rescue of him, but the impression he had of his captive was that he was a loner. Then he suddenly realized who the armed, shut-faced men must be. His fears subsided.

He raised his hands high. 'Boys!' he called out. 'You wouldn't cut loose at an old Mosby raider, would you?'

The man in the barn came out into the open, holding his rifle loosely in his right hand, followed by an older, worried-faced man. Luther took him to be the homesteader and could well understand his fretful look, harbouring wanted rebs within a few miles from a red-leg camp. Behind him he heard a girl's voice shout out, 'They're on their own, Pa!'

After giving him another searching look, the man from the barn said, 'You can step down, mister.' He glanced at Snake. 'I reckon you're a lawman the way that kid's trussed up; he don't look like your trail buddy, that's for sure.'

'You're right there, friend,' replied Luther, as he

swung down from his saddle. And don't you start feeling sorry for him, missee,' he said to the young, dark-haired girl standing looking at Snake. 'He may be just a kid, but he's a much wanted desperado.'

'Whatever you say he is,' Betty Anne said protestingly, 'he doesn't deserve to be tied up like a wild animal!'

Luther grinned at her. 'There is if I want to stay alive.' He picked up Snake's' rope. 'Come on, kid, I'll get you out of the sun into that barn and m'be you'll have the sense to have a drink. Then I can explain to these gents who I am and why I'm here.'

'I'll see that he has some water, Marshal,' Betty Anne said eagerly.

'Not until I see to it that he can't get up to any mischief in that barn,' Luther replied.

Betty Anne gave a loud disdaining snort and ran back into the house and by the time he had Snake sitting down, securely tied by one hand to a post, Betty Anne came into the barn carrying a jug of water and a glass. She was followed in by her father and the three holed-up rebs, still carrying their guns, still wary-eyed.

'See to the marshal's horse, Betty Anne,' Jethro ordered. 'And tell your ma to rustle up some extra chow. Go, girl! Do as I say! The kid's old enough to handle a jug of water on his own!'

Betty Anne glared at her pa, gave another loud sniff and ran out of the barn.

'What she can't hear she can't talk about,' Jethro said. He gave a twist of a grin. 'Those red-leg bastards have got me all nervy, Marshal. By the way I'm Jethro Lawson, owner of this piece of land, I'll leave these three gents to introduce themselves bein' this ain't like it's a social gatherin'.'

'I'm Billy Lang,' said the man who had been in the barn. 'The big fella is Joe Swain, him with the chest wound is Chuck Pearson. We rode with 'Bloody' Bill.' He gimlet-eyed Luther. 'Now it's your turn to unburden yourself, Marshal.'

'I'm Luther Kane, a Texas ranch straw boss,' Luther began. 'During the war I was a captain of a company of Colonel Mosby's raiders.' He grinned. 'Though I'm wearing a marshal's badge I'm not a genuine sworn-in lawman, but I was given this badge by Marshal Harper working out of Fort Smith.' He nodded in the direction of Snake. Still grinning he said, 'He's my first prisoner, though he kind of gave himself up to me.' Then he told them of why he'd had to leave Texas, of the men he had been forced to kill and about his crazy mission to take on the red legs by scotching their attempts to round up reb fugitives. In grim-faced silence the three rebs listened to what they were hearing. Luther gave a lopsided grin. 'I haven't worked out how I'm going to keep tabs on the red-leg troop yet, espcially now I've got a prisoner who I ought to take to Fort Smith so Judge Parker can hang him.'

The three rebs hard-eyed Snake. 'String the kid up here, Marshal; you've got the authority,' Billy Lang said. 'Then you can get on with what you think you oughta be doin'.'

Hearing that the man who had captured him wasn't really one of Judge Parker's manhunters, that he had been taken prisoner by a cowhand drifter, almost made Snake cry with shame. Then as Luther told of the killings he had to do, Snake had the savvy to realize he had stuck his head into a bear's cave trying to steal the big Texan's horse. And the looks the three ragged-assed saddle-bum characters were eyeing him with, frightened the crap out of him.

He had been too young to have fought in the war but he'd heard stories told by drunken old-timers in saloons of the men who had fought in the Southern guerilla bands, fast-shooting, big-pistol-wielding men who feared neither God nor the Devil. He wondered how much time he had left before the bastards slipped the noose around his neck. Snake suddenly had a great urge to have a drink of water.

Luther gave Snake another weighing up look then said, 'It's been a long, ball-aching day and I'm not up to conducting a hanging. If it's not putting you out any, Mr Lawson, me and my prisoner will spend a night in your barn here. I've got money to cover our chow and feed for the horse.' He would make his decision about asking the homesteader to hire him a horse when it was clear in his mind what he was going to do with Snake.

'You're welcome to stay, Marshal,' Jethro replied. He grinned. 'Betty Anne will welcome talking to a fella more her age, even though it seems likely the kid ain't goin' to get much older. That's if you've no objections, Marshal, bein' he's your prisoner.'

Luther agreed, albeit reluctantly, to Jethro's request, after all the man was putting himself out for him. Though he would have to make sure the girl kept well away from Snake. A man who could see a hanging rope swinging in front of his eyes would try any desperate measure to escape that fate – such as hurt the girl if she didn't free him.

'We're movin' out tomorrow,' Billy said. 'Chuck's fit enough to sit up on a horse again. That red-leg outfit is north of us so we oughta get a clear ride south. I hear there's a demand for gringo hard men in some quarters across the Rio Grande.' He grinned at Jethro. 'Once we've gone, Jethro, you'll be able to sleep restful in your bed once more. We're beholden to you and your good lady, especially Chuck, for givin' us shelter.'

'Haw, hell,' Jethro said with some embarrassment. 'If I hadn't took you in, Ma would have slung me outa the house. Now it's about time I finished off my chores. I want to get down to Mordue's stores early in the morning to pick up some supplies so Ma can fix you and your boys up with some rations that you can eat without stoppin' to make camp. Once you ride out, keep movin', Billy. Everyone in the Nations don't look kindly on "reb renegades".'

Betty Anne came into the barn carrying two bowls of steaming soup just as Luther was lighting the storm lantern. She gave Luther a sharp unkind look as she handed him a bowl of soup. Then she knelt down beside Snake and placed the other bowl at his side. 'Aren't you going to free his other arm, Marshal, so that he can eat his soup?' she snapped over her shoulder.

'Snake doesn't need two hands to tackle a bowl of soup!' Luther growled. Then the stress of all that had happened to him since leaving Texas got to him. 'I've told you once already that you haven't to feel sorry for Snake; he's a wanted killer!' he barked at her. 'If you want to show someone sympathy show it to me; that kid you're fretting over tried to Indian up on me and stick

80

a knife in my back! Now get yourself to bed where a young girl should be this time of the night!'

Luther heard the sound of Betty Anne's sobs until the clashing of the shack door cut them off.

'My, my,' grinned Snake. 'Ain't we in a twist!'

Luther savage-eyed him. 'Don't rile me any more than I am right now, Mr Whitney,' he said, his voice as menacing as his look. 'Or so help me I'll hang you for sure at sun-up! I ought to have shot you when you came at me with the knife. While I'm burdened with you, good men, men I fought alongside, could be in danger from those Union killers. Now you get to sleep, but before you drop off pray, if you still know to pray, that I'm not in a "twist" tomorrow!'

Snake knew he had crossed the invisible line that ran between him and the marshal. A foolhardy act that had brought him closer to his fearful fate. That depressing thought put him off his meal. Luther finished off his soup then walked across to Snake, saw that he hadn't touched his soup so he tied up his other hand, though loose enough for Snake to turn around in his sleep. He rolled out his blanket and sat on it with his back up against the gate of a stall. He took out one of his pistols, drew the hammer back at half-cock and laid it down close by his right leg. With one last look at Snake he tilted his hat over his eys and drifted off into a light sleep. The growing sickening pain in the pit of Snake's stomach prevented him from having any hope of sleep.

TEN

Jethro had finished loading his supplies on his flat bed at the rear of Mordue's stores, a large barn of a building where the river trail forked to the east, and walked into the store to give Mordue his due. He was surprised to see three red-leg troopers standing drinking and talking at the makeshift bar. On seeing him they stopped their talking to look at him with jaundiced-eyed stares. He indicated to Mordue who was stacking crates behind the bar that he wanted to see him at the loading bay.

'Those red legs frighten me, Mordue,' he said, as he handed the sutler the payment for his supplies. 'I can't stand being in the same territory as them, let alone in the same bar.'

Mordue grinned. 'They'll not put a scare in you for much longer, Jethro, their outfit is been ordered back to Fort Lawrence, Kansas, to be disbanded.'

'How did you come by that information?' a surprised Jethro asked.

'I may always look busy in my store when I've got drinkin' customers in,' the sutler said, grinning, 'but my ears are always flappin'. Now, according to those three at the bar, their capt'n ain't goin' back to Fort Lawrence, he's quit the army and he's told his men that he still intends to hunt down and hang reb scum – his words, not mine. And he'll personally pay any man who stays with him the same they're gettin' now. Those fellas are discussin' among themselves whether or not they should take up the capt'n's offer.'

Jethro didn't like what Mordue had told him. Not operating under the discipline, slight as it might be in the one-eyed captain's unit of the US Army, the bastard red legs would act as ruthlessly as a bunch of white bronco Indians. The only law along the Lodge Pole was administered by Marshal Harper and, dedicated lawman that he was, up against the marauding red legs was no law at all. Temporary Marshal Kane was loco if he thought he could carry on a running battle against them. There was one thing Jethro was happy about, the rebs he had been sheltering were leaving and the sooner he got back to the farm the quicker the threat hanging over him and his family would be lifted. With a hurried goodbye to Mordue, he practically leapt on to the wagon's seat and, picking up the reins, he kicked off the brake. The surprised whip-lashed-butted mule broke into an unaccustomed dust-raising gallop.

Luther kept a watchful eye on Snake freshening himself up at the horse tank. Betty Anne watched them from the shack doorway but made no attempt to come any closer to Snake. Luther reckoned that his message to her last night had got home, though in no way she was hiding her hateful feelings towards him. After he had dried himself, Snake came over to him with his hands outstretched for the binding ropes, all his former cockiness gone, accepting with his father's stoicism that Judge Parker was going to have his hanging.

Luther had come to a decision about Snake. He had asked Mrs Lawson where he could find the nearest town that had a sheriff and a jailhouse and when Jethro returned and the three reb fugitives had ridden off, he would take Snake there and hand him over to the sheriff with orders to contact Marshal Harper about whom he had in his jail. He had served the warrant the marshal had given him; he had done the hard part; Snake was in custody, so it was Marshal Harper's task to see that the kid got his just deserts. That would leave him free to do some marshalling, either side of the law, on behalf of the rebs being hunted down by the red legs.

Billy, Chuck and Joe had their horses all saddled up and were ready to ride out as soon as Jethro returned with their promised rations, and they had said their final goodbyes to him and his family. Luther had roped Snake back on to the post in the barn and had joined the three rebs to have a few words with them before they rode south. The rattling speed of the approaching wagon drew all their attentions.

'Jesus'! breathed Billy. 'Jethro's sure makin' that old mule step out! I hope the red legs ain't followin' in that wagon's dust trail!'

The hands of three anxious-faced men reached for booted rifles.

'Don't get alarmed, boys,' Luther said. 'I'm the law around here, not that one-eyed, red-leg captain.'

'That's m'be so, Marshal,' replied Billy 'but it won't hurt any to be prepared in case that capt'n thinks otherwise.'

'You can put away your rifles, boys!' Jethro called out as he yanked the mule to an ass-sliding halt. 'I ain't bein' trailed. It's just that I've heard some not so good news about those red legs who are billetted in that army post. It won't affect you boys now you're movin' out of the territory.' Dismounting he told them about the red leg captain quitting the army and forming a gang of regulators.

'What the captain intends doing could work in my favour, Jethro,' Luther said, thoughtfully. 'He'll be riding at the head of a bunch of lawbreakers, shoot-on-sight outlaws. And I can do that with the full backing of Judge Parker's authority.'

'If only half of the capt'n's detail stand by him,' Billy said, 'you'll have m'be ten, twelve men to gun down, Marshal. Now the odds will come down somewhat in your favour if you had three unpaid deputies ridin' with you.' He looked at Chuck and Joe. 'Ain't that so, boys?'

'Dead right, Billy,' replied Chuck, with an affirmitive nod from Joe. 'It ain't never been in our nature to show our backs to those red-leg sonsuvbitches but in this case we were forced to,' Chuck continued. 'We're not listed as wanted men by the law here in the Nations but we would have been if we started shootin' down men in blue-belly uniforms; that's trouble me and the boys couldn't handle.' He grinned at Luther. 'Now it will be just like it was durin' the war: we can shoot them down like the mad dogs they are.'

Snake, listening to all the talking going on, began to

wonder what sort of men these former reb fighters were. His philosophy was uncomplicated: look out for number one and to hell with anyone else. Now he was hearing that three ragged-assed fugitives were willing to stand alongside the marshal in his battle against the red legs, against odds three times their strength. And not for any cash gain, like risking your hide to rob a bank or a stage, but because they didn't like being pushed around. Pride, Snake reckoned, his pa and his people must have had when the whites grabbed their lands. A pride that got his pa and half his tribe killed. He didn't believe in letting pride, or whatever it was, get you an early grave. Being a loner was easier on his mind.

'Rider comin' along the river trail,' Billy said, and rifles were raised again.

'It's OK, it's Marshal Harper,' Luther said. Then he knew exactly what he should do about Snake.

He hurried across to Betty Anne standing at the shack door. His saying, 'Go to the barn and free Snake!' changed her scowl into a look of surprise. Luther handed her his small calibre pistol. 'Give him this, but tell him that if he crosses my trail again I'll kill him, OK?' Betty Anne, slack-jawed with disbelief didn't move. 'Go, girl, pronto!' Luther almost yelled. 'Before Marshal Harper rides in!'

A tear smiling Betty Anne reached up on her toes and kissed Luther on the cheek, and it was Luther's turn to look surprised. Then, in a flurry of skirt-raised dust, she dashed over to the barn.

'Are you goin' soft, Luther?' Billy asked with a grin when Luther rejoined them.

Luther shook his head. 'I've a feeling we're going to

have our bellies full of killing in the next few weeks, Billy,' he replied. 'I don't want a kid who don't know right from wrong to be added to that list. And I never had the stomach for a hanging, even out-and-out cattle lifters.'

'Well I'll be. . . .' Marshal Harper said as he drew up his horse and caught sight of Luther. 'I figured you'd be well on your way to Fort Smith with your prisoner by now.' The marshal looked about him. 'I can't see no prisoner; is he in the barn?'

'No, he isn't, Marshal,' Luther said. 'I let him go. He saved my life by stabbing the bastard who tried to bush-whack me so I was beholden to him. But that's not the reason I turned him loose. He killed a man who had raped his granddaughter and that's not murder in any fair-minded man's book.' Luther straight-eyed the marshal 'I know it wasn't legal what I did, so if you want your badge back you've only got to ask for it.'

Marshal Harper thought that there was some sense in Luther's action in freeing his prisoner. 'Naw, you keep your badge, Marshal Kane,' he said. 'You did what you thought what was right, that's all a man can do.' And it wasn't as though old Judge Parker was short of candidates to swing on his gallows, he thought.

'Now I'll tell you about the big trouble building up in your bailiwick, Marshal,' Luther continued.

Marshal Harper's face got longer and meaner as Luther told him about the red-leg captain's decision to wage a private war against the reb hold-outs in the Nations, and what he intended to do to scotch the captain's actions.

'Jesus Christ!' the marshal gasped. 'It would be worse

than a damned range war! As if the territory wasn't wild enough!' He cast a wondering-eyed look at the three rebs. 'If you don't mind me sayin' so, Luther, you ain't got much of an army.'

Luther cold-smiled. 'It'll do. There wasn't many of us fighting alongside Colonel Mosby but he taught us how to fight sneaky, Indian-like.'

'Well, every law-abidin' citizen has the right to to defend himself if attacked by this captain and his vigilantes, or whatever they call themselves. And the law here in the Nations will back you up.' He looked apologetically at Luther. 'That's me!'

'That's all we want to hear, Marshal,' replied Luther. 'We don't want to make ourselves wanted men and have to fight the law as well. And no offence to you, Marshal, but stick to serving your warrants on wanted owlhoots, keep out of our fight. The settling up of old scores can be a messy, bloody business and these boys have a lot of settling up to do.'

'I'll do that, Luther,' Marshal Harper said. 'And no offence taken.' He grinned. 'I'm too old in the tooth and set in my ways to be a wild-ass brush boy.' He twisted round in his saddle and, raising his voice, called out, 'Is that fresh coffee I can smell brewin' in there, Mrs Lawson?'

Mrs Lawson stepped out on to the porch. 'It sure is, Marshal, you come inside and let those boys go about their business.' Then she walked back indoors.

Mrs Lawson knew that her decision to put up the three rebs on the farm had caused Jethro a lot of sleepless nights and he wouldn't stop worrying until they had left. Now the rebs were about to leave and what they intended doing had her worried that they could be riding out to their deaths. But she had been raised as a plainswoman, and from a very early age she had seen men ride out on some pretext or other and never return.

Snake scrambled up the hillside still pondering over the reason the big Texan had let him go. He had to go back a long way before he could recollect anyone doing him a favour, and no way as big as saving him from a hanging. When he had heard that Marshal Harper was riding in what slight hopes he'd had of getting the better of Marshal Kane on the trail to Fort Smith faded. He had heard of no outlaw escaping from Marshal Harper's custody.

At first, when Betty Anne had come rushing into the barn and cut his bounds with a sharp tool he thought that the freeing of him had been her own idea, kind of feeling sorry for him being he was all set to meet the hangman. When, as she handed him a pistol, she told him that it was Marshal Kane's doing, he couldn't believe it. Though he believed the marshal's warning that he would shoot him on sight if they met up again. The Texan had given him a break, for what reason Snake couldn't figure out, probably that he and the three hillbillies would have their hands full taking on a bunch of red legs. Whatever it was didn't matter, he was free.

'Go out by the back way, Snake,' Betty Anne said. 'There's a brush-filled gully that leads up on to the high ground. It should give you cover until you reach the crest.' She smiled lightly. 'I'm sorry I couldn't get you a horse.'

'That's no matter, Betty Anne,' Snake said. Then grinned at her. 'I couldn't take on any more luck.' Though a horse would have come in handy, he thought, and a belt of reloads for the pistol. But Snake knew it was pinch-assed thinking. He was free and lived by his wits and the gun; he had both, he would get by.

Then he had another pleasant surprise. Betty Anne kissed him on the cheek as he stepped through the back doorway. Crouching low, he ran across to the gully with Betty Anne repeating Marshal Kane's warning ringing in his ears.

As Snake topped the ridge, still keeping low, he caught the tangy smell of cheap tobacco smoke and dropped nose to the dirt. Then came the snuffling and wind-breaking of horses. He drew back the hammer of the Colt ready to fight off any trouble he could have landed in. He didn't remember even seeing his Indian pa, but he silently thanked his memory for passing on some of his tracking and hunting skills that must have come his way through his Comanche bloodline.

Crawling closer to where he judged the horses to be, he saw that there were three mounts, saddled up and with rifles in the boots. Saved from a hanging, a kiss from a pretty girl, now a mount just waiting for him to leap on its back. Snake grinned. He had never had such a lucky day. Then through the thickets he saw the legs of one of the riders of the horses, wearing blue army pants tucked into red leather boots. Apart from unknowingly trying to steal one of their horses, Snake had kept well clear of the red-leg patrols in his lawless activities, well aware that they were mean-minded, hair-triggered sons-of-bitches, not favourably inclined to

Indians and 'breeds. And he was putting some distance between himself and them right now. He began to sidle back along the ridge, forgetting about his need to grab hold of a horse. Then an unusual niggling inside him stopped his crawling when he thought that the red legs could only be watching what was going on down on the farm and the only interest to them would be the three rebs and Marshal Kane. Snake was beginning to have a conscience; he was thinking of the well-being of some-one other than himself. He began to work his way along to the red legs again.

'I don't know who that big fella is next to the paint,' said Langley, one of the red legs who had been drink-ing in the sutler's, store, but those black-whiskered saddle-tramps are ex-brush boys or my name ain't Josh Langley.'

'M'be they're part of the bunch we broke up a week ago, Josh,' Denny replied. 'I know I winged one of the high-tailin' bastards. All those backwoods boys look alike, but the way one of them is sittin' awkward like on his horse he could the one I put lead into.'

'They seem to be ready to move out,' Nate, the third red leg said. 'If we don't want to lose them again we oughta find a place to bushwhack the bastards.' He fierce grinned. 'If the other fella is ridin' with them then he'll get the same treatment. Then we can ride back to the post and let the capt'n know we're willin' to soldier on with him. Give him the good news that we've already fired the first shots and that there's three rebs less to hunt down.'

Snake hadn't heard the red-legs conversation but he didn't need it written down for him what was in their minds as the three rode past him with their rifles held across their saddle horns. If he'd had a rifle he would have back shot them without any feeling of guilt. The least he could do was to warn the marshal and his buddies of the trap they were riding into. His pa's people, Snake thought, with a hint of pride, would call it settling a debt of honour.

Snake stepped out of the brush right in front of Luther's horse as the four riders came up out of the valley, and found himself covered by four pistols. In his short, but wild life thieving in the bad lands along the Kansas border he had seen some quick reaction men, but these four were in a class of their own, men who must sleep with both eyes open.

'I thought you would have been hot-footing it to Kansas by now!' Luther said, angrily. 'I gave you your freedom and by hell it's only by a whisker me or the boys didn't shoot you dead. What are you doing here?'

'Save your lead for those three red legs up ahead apiece, Marshal,' Snake said. 'I saw them watchin' you from up here. Then they rode along the trail with their rifles out. I ain't had any schoolin' but I've figured out that they'll be hunkered down in the rock fall just around the bend there waitin' to pick you off.'

Luther and the rebs exchanged worried-eyed glances. 'And I was aiming to pick the time and place we were going to start the war,' Luther said.

'It could be the same red legs Jethro saw in the stores, Luther,' Bill said.

'Wherever they've come from they've got us at a disadvantage,' Luther replied. 'We can't let them shoot us and we can't not shoot all three of them, if we don't want the one-eyed captain alerted that the fellas he's hunting are much closer than he thought.'

'You'll never flush them out, Marshal,' Snake said. 'It's a tangle of rocks there; you won't know what piece of rock to look behind and the bastards ain't goin' to allow you to do that!' Then Snake surprised himself by saying, 'If one of you gents will loan me his rifle I could kinda ease them out into the open.' He grinned cheekily. 'Then if you hillbillies are as dead-eyed-Dick with your guns as I've heard tell, you oughta put paid to them without raisin' too much sweat.'

Billy leaned forward in his saddle and flint-eyed Snake. 'We're good, Bub,' he grated, 'or we wouldn't be still ridin' around. Are you as good is the question? Or are you just a blowhard kid after makin' a rep for himself as a hard man?'

Before Snake, stung by the insult, could protest that he could do what he said he could do, Luther butted in.

'The kid's got a dead or alive flyer out on him,' he said. 'And according to Marshal Harper he's a bona-fide killer as young as he is.'

Snake, his dander up, turned his righteous anger on to Luther. 'I ain't denying I'm a horse-thief and a road agent, but them fellas I shot were lawbreakers like me and who were tryin' to kill me! And I shot them face to face!'

Luther grinned. 'All right, Snake, simmer down, but we're playing for big stakes here, our lives no less, and we've been playing this game for a hell of a long time and we're getting weary of it. So you can see why Billy is a mite tetchy.' He drew his Winchester from its boot and handed it down to Snake. 'OK, boy, you do your thing, show us where the sonsuvbitches are and we'll do the rest. But don't take too long to do it in case those red legs get wondering why we haven't ridden into their trap. We'll be ready in position to send them to hell in ten minutes. And take care, you're being hunted by the law, don't get the red legs on your trail as well.'

Snake hefted the rifle a couple of times then he levered a shell into the chamber. 'My pa was a Comanche chief,' he said. 'He named me Little Black Snake.' He grinned at Luther. 'The sonsuvbitches in those rocks are about to have their asses bitten by a sidewinder.' In a blur of movement Snake disappeared into the brush.

'Were we as cocksure when we were kids, Billy?' Chuck asked.

'I don't recollect ever bein' a kid,' replied Billy. 'A bunch of that crackpot abolitionist John Brown's free-staters burnt down our shack, killin' my ma and pa. Why, I don't rightly know, because we kept no slaves. Pa's piece of dirt hardly produced enough to feed us. The next thing I knew I was wearing a big Colt that took all my fourteen-year-old strength to hold and fire when I rode with Quantrill's wild bunch to put a torch to Lawrence, Kansas, long before the big war started.'

'OK boys,' Luther said. 'We've all got happy memories. Let's get down to do what we're going to do.' He gave a twist of a smile. 'We don't want Little Black Snake to think we're a bunch of over-the-hill farts. Billy, you and Joe get down on to the bottom land on foot, until you're well clear of the rocky stretch of the ridge. Then come up and cross the trail and work your way back to the rocks and wait for the kid to do his flushing out. Me and Chuck will come in from this side. So between us we should have those red legs boxed in when the firing opens up.'

Chuck grinned. 'The bastards won't know who's ambushin' who.'

Snake paused just below the crest for a breather and to eye the rocks and shale slides that stretched 300 yards or so to the thin brown ribbon of the trail. On leaving the rebs, he had climbed straight up the steep slope with the speed of a sure-footed mountain goat, his pa's Indian pride being at stake. He had crossed over to the far side of the ridge and, still keeping up his lung bursting pace, ran along until instead of running through grass and brush, he felt the hardness of rock beneath his feet. He stopped in mid stride. If the rocky strata ran true on the ridge the red legs would be bedded down somewhere on the other side. It was finding-out time.

Snake looked long and hard but could see no signs of the ambushers though he knew they would be well within rifle range of the trail. Moving down the slope until he spotted either of them was too risky of him being seen by the red legs. And by the time they gave their positions away by their rifle flashes he would be dead.

Snake suddenly ceased his frustrated frowning and grinned. Maybe he couldn't flush them out, he thought, but a land slip could. Not a yard in front of him was a decent sized boulder perched at the head of a wide swathe of rocks and shale which, in the shimmering-heat haze, seemed to be sliding downwards already. He stretched out with both feet and pushed hard. The rock was more loosely balanced than he had thought and he almost followed it down the grade. It barrelled its way downwards, picking up speed, friction dragging great patches of shale in its wake until it seemed to Snake that the whole side of the ridge was hurtling down to the trail. It was now safe for him to climb down and shoot any red leg he saw as they scattered to escape being crushed – if he could see them through the dust kicked up by the landslide.

Josh was the first to break cover. He had heard the thunder-like noise and saw the wall of rocks and dust rolling down on him. Wild-eyed, he scrambled over to the rocks to his left out of the path of the avalanche. Chuck, lying across a boulder, had him in his rifle sights. He held back squeezing the trigger until the red leg saw that he hadn't run free from danger after all. The Winchester kicked twice against Chuck's shoulder and Death caught up with Josh, and he fell backwards with two shells in his chest. Arms and legs flapped loosely as his body rolled downwards, causing his own rock slip before ending up in a crumpled heap on the edge of the trail.

Denning had further to run and only by a few feet did he avoid the bone crushing wave of rocks. Luther saw him come stumbling through the dust, coughing and spluttering and before the red leg fully realized he was clear of the avalanche he shot him. The smashing impact of the close range shot flung Denny back into the dust clouds out of Luther's sight. Through the dust, Luther could still hear the rocks thundering down so it was more than a fair chance that if his shot hadn't killed the red leg, the rocks would have.

Nate, in the centre of the rock face, hadn't much of a chance to escape his fate. On hearing the fearful roar above him, he had dropped his rifle and made a run for it, but in his panic-stricken dash he had broken his right ankle slipping between two rocks. He only had time to make a few painful, stumbling steps, and a horrified scream before being engulfed by the avalanche.

Snake, picking his way down the now shale-cleared slope, saw a half buried body. He hadn't heard any sounds of the shooting above the deafening roar of the falling rocks so with the dust haze rapidly dispersing in the strong wind, he kept his rifle raised and watched for any sighting of the other two red legs.

Then he heard the marshal yell, 'Come on down, kid. We've shot two of them; I reckon the third one didn't get clear of the rocks.'

'Yeah, he's up here!' he shouted back. He cut across the face of the ridge to avoid the high bank of rocks and shale that lay at the foot of the ridge, spilling down as far as the river's edge.

'Good work, Snake,' Luther said, as he reached the trail and three rebs favoured him with congratulatory grins.

'They'll also have "Wanted for blocking the Lodge Pole trail" on your flyer, Snake,' Billy said.

'That's our cue to get away from here,' Luther said. 'Before someone comes along to find out what all the noise was about. Did you see those fellas' horses, Billy? I didn't pass them.'

'They're OK, Luther,' replied Billy. 'They were hitched up well clear of the kid's mountain-moving trick. But the noise scared them and they broke free and headed in the direction of the army post. When they ride in without their riders it will set that one-eyed captain ponderin' more than somewhat.'

'We ought to get close enough to him to see what he comes up with when he finds out what's happened to his men,' Luther said. He turned to face Snake. 'I was hoping to get you a mount so you could be on your way. It seems that you'll have to make Kansas on foot.' He grinned. 'Though for a noted horse-thief like yourself it shouldn't be a hard job grabbing a horse.'

'I'd like to tag along with you boys, Marshal,' Snake said, surprising himself again. A loner, riding alongside three old reb guerilla fighters and a marshal? He could be wearing a lawman's badge next. 'There could be some more flushin' out to do,' he said straight-faced. 'Of course, Marshal, you could be thinkin' that it ain't fittin' that a killer you oughta be escortin' to Fort Smith to be strung up, should ride with you as a pard.'

Luther gave Snake a long, judging look. Before he had successfully flushed out the three red legs the kid had already proved that he must have the skills of a brush raider to have kept out of the law's hands. Skills, he thought, he couldn't afford to turn away, considering the odds they were facing.

'Riding with us could get you killed sooner than later,' Luther told him, still feeling that he hadn't the right to involve Snake in shooting trouble he'd had no part in.

Snake laughed. 'You've already told me that good news, marshal. If Marshal Harper grabs me I'm as good as dead.' His face hardened. 'If I'm goin' to die,

Marshal, I'd like it to be quick by the bullet, not bein'
choked to death in public!'

'What do you think boys?' Luther asked, looking at
his small command.

Billy, speaking as spokesman for Chuck and Joe, said,
'I reckon he'll be able to pull his weight ridin' with us,
Luther. As long as he don't keep wreckin' the real estate
on the way. By the way, Snake, the fella I shot had a rifle
with him; it could be lyin' close by his body just there.'
He pointed out to Snake just where the body was.

Snake climbed back up the slope and in a matter of
minutes came back grinning, holding a rifle and a well-
filled gunbelt and holstered pistol.

'That's you armed up, Snake,' Luther said, thrusting
his second pistol Snake had handed back to him into
the top of his pants. 'Now we'll see about getting you a
horse as soon as we can. We might have to hightail it out
of a bad situation and though I reckon your Comanche
pa was as they say, fleet of foot, and he's passed some of
that speed on to you, you can't move as speedily as a
horse under the whip.'

'I can scout ahead on foot, Marshal,' Snake said.
'We're not too far away from that army post the red legs
use and I know the trail ahead, all twistin' and dog-leg
bends. You wouldn't know you'd run into a bunch of
red legs until your horses bumped noses.'

Luther did some rapid thinking. What Snake had
said made sense and they would need all the edge they
could get.

'You take point, Snake,' he said. 'But,' he warned, 'If
you see any red legs you come back to us, fast, savvy?
Don't be dumb-assed foolish and try to take them on

your own. We don't want that red-leg captain knowing that he's got trouble coming his way. We're taking on big odds so when we fight them I want it to be the way I planned, OK?'

Holding the fully loaded rifle and gunbelt fastened across his waist, Snake was more than keen to show his worth to his new *compadres* and move out as point man. 'OK, Marshal,' he said and, gripping the rifle in his right hand, set off along the trail in a loping, ground-eating strlde.

ELEVEN

Captain Chartris, still in full dress uniform, though he was no longer a serving officer in the US Army, cast a combat-experienced eye over his new command. It was only ten men strong, with the possibility of three more recruits when they returned from a drinking session at the sutler's stores. Though they were good men and, like himself, had a personal burning hatred for the reb irregulars, and had been willing to serve under him as civilian vigilantes to erase some of their hatred.

Many of them had had kinfolk killed, or burnt out, by Missouri brush boys along the Kansas-Missouri border lands, longways before the war, in the fearsome days when the no-quarter-given fighting between the free-staters and the pro-slavers gave Kansas its infamous name 'Bleeding' Kansas. The captain's lips tightened into two hard lines. With the Lord's help he would strike down the rebs who were still hiding out in the Nations with all the furious fervour and blood letting old John Brown had wielded against the reb border ruffians. This section of the Nations would shed blood as Kansas had done, only this time it would be all reb blood. All in all, the captain thought, he was well satis-fied with the weapon he had at hand with which to strike the slavers.

On quitting the army, the men had handed in their uniform tunics and were now fully dressed as civilians. He would keep wearing his uniform till the last of the rebs were dead, or they had killed him. The commissary major at the post had fought in the same regiment during the war as he had, and held the same views towards the rebs, and by some dubious ledger work on the post's personnel roll, allowed them to keep their army horses and their gear.

With all of them now being civilians they had to leave the post and were now billeted in some deserted build-ings that had once been the house and barns of a worked-out farm. The captain didn't expect to spend much time here, but it would do as a base for their few supplies, and resting place for the men after several days of day and night patrolling hunting the rebs, and provided a roof over their heads.

'Barker!' he called out. 'As soon as those three men show up, and we know whether or not they wish to ride with us, send out scouting details. Tell them to ask at the usual places, bars, cat-houses, farms, whatever, if they have had any sightings of ragged-assed men riding along back trails. Tell them also not to forget to mention the substantial bounty if their information leads to the apprehension of any reb renegades.'

Barker grinned at the captain. 'There's so-called men here in the Nations who would sell their closest kin for a fistful of ready cash.' Though he was no longer a sergeant and wore no uniform he gave Captain

Chartris a smart military salute, then spun round on his heels shouting out orders. Civilians or not, he thought, the old army discipline had to be maintained, the captain would expect no less of him.

'The kid's comin' back in, Luther,' Billy yelled out. Without another word being spoken, the four of them split up, two either side of the trail, rifles out of their boots, ready to fight off any trouble that could be coming along Snake's back trail.

'It's OK, boys,' Luther replied. 'Snake doesn't seem to be in a hurry so he's not the bearer of bad news!'

Snake came up to Luther. 'The trail's clear,' he said. 'But the army post is only a few hundred yards ahead and I reckon you oughta cut across into the bottom lands. There's places there where you can lie up, outa sight, yet still be able to see all the comin's and goin's at the post. It'll be rough goin' because there ain't no regular trails through that wilderness.'

Billy took a long look at the wind-waving area of cane, weeds and brush that stretched as far as he could see along the Lodge Pole, then he looked down at Snake.

'Why Snake,' he said, trying hard to keep the smile off his face, 'I can see traces runnin' through that wilderness that look like well-trodden turnpikes to the tracks that ran through the backwoods where I once farmed.'

Snake, knowing he was being ribbed, took it in good part. He also knew that he had been accepted as an equal by the Missouri hard men – as long as he didn't let them down, he thought soberly.

They made camp on a dry pad of higher ground with a clear opening through the undergrowth where, by using army glasses, they could keep the post under observation. It was Joe's turn to stand the first watch. The rest were eating their share of the still warm food that Mrs Lawson had baked for them. Their next meals would be cold and eaten out of a can, which to all of them, including Snake, wasn't an unusual occurrence.

Luther, as he ate, was trying to come up with some plan of action again. They couldn't sit out in this wilderness any length of time as they would soon run out of rations, or risk been spotted from the post. And it was an impossibility to attack the red legs while they were in the army post. Finally, but reluctantly, he had to favour his original decision of letting the red legs make the first move, hoping it would be soon, then play it out as it came. Joe's soft call of 'Something's about to happen at the post, Luther!' had him cease his worrying and crawl up to the look-out point.

Joe handed Luther the glasses. 'That freight wagon you can see has just hauled in one of those dead red legs. I reckon it's the fella Chuck downed. A coupla blue-bellies carried it into that building with the flag flyin' on its chimney.'

Luther, glasses fixed on the post, said, 'Now we should see some action from that red-leg captain, Joe. He'll not take kindly to seeing one of his boys shot dead and wondering what's happened to the other two.' Suddenly he lowered the glasses and gave Joe a puzzled look. 'A trooper has just rode out of the post and headed north, fast, but he wasn't a red leg! Wait a minute, didn't Jethro tell us how he heard those red legs in the sutler's talking about their captain quitting the army and raising up a band of vigilantes?' he exclaimed.

'Yeah,' replied Joe. Then, realizing the significance of Luther's remarks, cursed. 'We're watchin' the wrong mouse-hole, Luther. The captain and his boys ain't billeted in the post and that rider's goin' to where he is to tell him about the dead red leg.'

Luther gave Joe the glasses and told him to keep watching the post and then he crept back to the camp. He told them the bad news then spoke to Snake.

'Snake,' he said. 'You claim you know your way around the territory, is there a spot where a bunch of men could make camp, not too far away? I mean a permanent site with buildings, good water? The impression I got of the captain, in the short time I saw him, is a man who doesn't go off at half-cock. He'll plan his actions as though it was a full-blown military operation, which they are to him. So he'll want a base to operate from, cover for his men and their horses when they're resting up after a patrol, and a sheltered place for what supplies he's got.'

Snake gave a sheepish grin. 'When I said I knew the territory hereabouts, Marshal, I forgot to mention I mostly saw it from low down on the back of a dust-raisin' horse chased by a posse and hadn't much time to take in the scenery. But, if I recollect right, there are some abandoned buildings a few miles north of here.'

'OK, boys,' Luther said. 'We'll move out and check

these buildings. Once we find out where the red legs are the sooner we'll know how many of the sonsuvbitches we're facing.'

TWELVE

Captain Chartris thought that Major Catlin, the post's commander, had sent the news that one of his former men had been killed, and two more probably lying dead under a rock fall, to let him know that he need no longer postpone his private war against the reb renegades as his command was at full strength. A tragic accident, he had thought. That was soon dispelled as the messenger finished his report.

'It was Josh Langley's body the mule-skinner brung in, Capt'n,' the trooper continued. 'Though the body was knocked about somewhat by the rocks, Josh was killed by a gunshot.'

'Shot!' The captain sprang to his feet and leaned across the crate that did service as his table, eyes gleaming with anger. 'Are you certain?'

'Beggin' the capt'n's pardon,' the trooper replied. 'I've seen bullet wounds before and Josh had two, plumb in his chest.'

'Yes . . . well . . . I apologize.' The captain was lost for words. The news of the shooting had struck him like a blow in the face. The rebs' unexpected attack had made him look a fool. He had made a basic military error: he had underestimated his enemy. He dismissed the messenger and told him to thank the major for notifying him of the serious turn of events, then began buckling on his sword and pistol belt. He looked across at Barker, face set in rigid lines of cold anger. It was a look that sent shivers down the ex-sergeant's spine; he had served with the captain on many a killing raid and was well aware of his many moods, but not the one he was seeing now.

'Those reb scum have thrown down the gauntlet, Barker,' the captain said, his voice in control of its anger as his face was. 'And by God we'll pick it up! I'll see every one of those renegades shot dead or hanged, and that's not a promise but a fact! Have the men ready to move out in fifteen minutes, Barker. We'll ride at full strength to where this avalanche occurred, making sure we're not riding into an ambush. Though I think it's highly unlikely. Those brush trash are hit-and-run raiders. But I'm not taking any chances. Once we have seen Wilson and Locke decently buried, we'll carry out my original plan of campaign, sending out patrols asking for information about the whereabouts of any suspected rebs.'

'Capt'n,' Barker replied. 'Once the troop hears of the three boys bein' shot down they'll be ready to move out in five minutes, armed ready for bear!'

The captain smiled, though it was as icy as his look. 'Hate, Barker,' he said, 'kind of hones a man's fighting capabilities. And those rebs who killed our comrades are going to find just how sharp it is.'

*

THE JAYHAWKERS

With the trail veering away from the Lodge Pole, Luther and his men had to leave the sheltering cover of the wet lands and risk riding along the main trail. As a precaution, with the trail narrowing between high bluffs, Snake was walking point again. When Snake came back this time from point he was running and waving his arms. When he came closer to them they heard his shout of 'Riders comin', clear the trail!'

In a matter of seconds, Luther and the Missourians had forced their horses through a thick stand of timber on their left of the trail. Snake, with no horse to worry about, took shelter in the long grass opposite them, thinking that if he had to make a run for it, the wet lands were not far behind him.

The red-leg column, with the captain leading, thundered past them, neither looking to their left or right.

Chuck grinned at Luther. 'It looks as though that one-eyed captain has got the news about the sudden demise of three of his boys. He's down to ten men, Luther.'

'By killing those red legs we dented the captain's pride somewhat, Chuck.' Luther replied. 'Now he knows that the men he's hunting are capable of fighting back, hurting him, and that he's got a small war on his hands. Something the captain didn't reckon on. Could kinda throw him off balance and allow us to hit him again with no risk to us. As you say, Chuck, they'll be riding to the rock slide to see to the burying of those two still there, so we will have to try and get close to them to find out what the captain's next moves are.'

'That'll take some doin', Luther,' Chuck said. 'After the next bend, the trail opens up and those bastards

109

will be mite apprehensive, castin' glances every which way, thinkin' they're about to be fired on.'

'Young Snake, using his pa's Indian blood, could get in real close to them without raising an alarm,' Luther said. He dismounted and walked back through the trees to the edge of the trail and called across to Snake to come over and join them.

'Do you think you can do it, Snake?' Luther asked after he had explained to him the importance of them finding out in which direction the red legs would ride once they had seen to the burial of the two bodies.

'They could come back this way, Snake,' he said. 'Or ride south, or cut across the ridge line and head west. It would be raising no sweat on our part to pick up their trail, but that captain will be making sure his men aren't jumped again; he'll more than likely leave a man here and there to watch his back trail. We'll have to be smarter, such as getting ahead of him so we can sort of surprise the sonsuvbitches like we did on the ridge, so we can leave him to bury a few more of his men. By such-like tactics we can whittle down his outfit until at last we can meet him on equal terms, face him in the open.'

Luther gave Snake what he believed was how his pa would have smiled when he gave the order to strike at a white-eyes' wagon-train.

'Then,' Luther continued, 'that one-eyed captain will know that the war is finally over for him, the hard way. I'll come with you as far as it is safe to do so to give you some covering fire if you've got to get to hell out of it fast. As I told you before I don't want you take them on all on your own.'

Snake beamed at his hard-faced partners, violent men who had been forced to live by the gun, and yet possessing a sense of loyalty to each other his Indian pa would have understood, as he did now. It gave him a surprisingly good feeling.

'Yeah, I can do that, Luther,' he said, for the first time calling the marshal by his name. After all, he thought, we're all partners now. Until the death, he added soberly. 'Though I'd be obliged if one of you pards could loan me a knife.' He grinned at Luther. 'I kinda misplaced mine back along the trail apiece. Your big pig sticker would be welcome, Chuck.'

Chuck grinned at him. 'You ain't picked up your pa's heathen ways, have you, Snake, liftin' white-eyes' hair?'

'No, Chuck,' Snake replied. 'It's just that a blade could come in useful if I get into a tight spot. Knifin' a fella is a damn sight quieter than loosing a pistol off at him. That racket could bring the whole bunch of red legs down on me.'

Chuck thought that he had started his killing days early but the way Snake had spoken he must have been shooting and knifing before he was big enough to get astride a horse. 'Yeah,' he said. 'I can see a situation where a bowie could come in handy, Snake, you're welcome to it.' He drew out the broad-bladed knife from its sheath and handed it to Snake.

'You three boys stay here in the timber,' Luther said. 'If things go wrong for me and Snake don't come fire-ballin' along to help us out. You'll only get yourselves gunned down as well, for damn all. I don't want that captain to think that there's more than two rebs

111

responsible for the killing of his men.' Luther hard-eyed the Missourians. 'Then, when you judge it's the right time, you show the captain how wrong he's been, OK?'

The three weren't happy about having to stay behind, but they knew that Luther was right. Mad-ass, unthought-out attacks against an enemy over twice their strength went against all their guerilla fighting tactics, and they gave Luther reluctant nods of accep-tance of his orders.

Luther turned to Snake. 'OK, boy, let's go scouting.'

Luther stayed well back, picking out the red legs bunched at the rock slide with his army glasses. Even rein-leading his horse across the arid flats to get in closer would raise dust. He could get nearer to the red legs like Snake was attempting, on foot, but if Snake got into trouble he would not only have to give him the backing of a fast firing Winchester, but the chance of a fast getaway, doubling up with him on his horse. Two men haring it on foot had no chance at all of escaping from being shot dead. He knee'd the horse down into a dried-out water hole, pulling out his Winchester before dismounting. He squatted down on the rim of the hole and looked across the heat shimmering plain, ears alert for the distant sound of gunfire that would be the grim warning that Snake had run into trouble.

Snake was belly crawling along a shallow slash in the land that he guessed, in the wet season, must be one of the many rain channels running down from the ridge, which now after a quick glance, was no more than a hundred ahead of him. Though wringing with sweat

Snake was in his element, pitting his wits against the enemy, which would normally be Judge Parker's marshals and town sheriffs' posses.

Several more minutes of crawling and he noticed that the gully had widened and deepened as it began to climb the ridge. He stopped and raised his head again, peering through tufts of sun-baked yellowed grass. Two red legs were standing at the on the edge of the land-slip halfway up the slope, close enough to hear one of them shout, 'We've found Locke, Capt'n! We'll bring him down!'

Captain Chartris gazed narrow-eyed up at the ridge, picturing exactly what had happened here. If he hadn't already known that Langley had been shot he knew that the rock slide hadn't been an act of God. His three men had set up an ambush for an unknown number of reb fugitives, but somehow they knew of the trap and started a landslip and shot his men down as they ran for safety. But what was done was done, the captain thought. What was important now was to find out how many rebs there were, and where the murderous bastards were now. The two riflemen he had up on the ridge would at least make sure the rebs kept their distance until they had done what they had come here for, to see the dead had decent Christian burials.

'The rebs must have come up from the south, Barker,' he said. 'The trail passes close to a holding, if I recollect rightly. Take a man and ask the owner if he has seen riders, strangers to him, using the trail within the last few days.' Hard-eyed, he added, 'Question him real closely, Barker, make sure he isn't telling you false. As we have discovered there're still many reb sympathizers in the territory.'

'Never fear, Capt'n,' replied Baker grimly. 'I'll question that sodbuster real closely, Langley was an old wartime buddy of mine and I want to see the bastards who killed him just as dead.'

'Good,' said the captain. 'It's imperative we find out just how many rebs were responsible for this.' He chin pointed in the direction of the landslip. 'Once I've seen to the burying of Wilson and Logan I intend splitting up the troop. I and three men will ride westwards to Plattsville and start asking questions there. The rest of the troop are to head along the Lodge Pole trail north and once they've checked out the farms and odd ranches this side of the Kansas border on possible sightings of any reb fugitives they'll swing south again and meet up with me at Plattsville. You ride there too after you've gleaned what you can from the farmer. What intelligence we get can be discussed and a plan of campaign against the rebs put into action.'

The captain's face twisted in anger as he punched his saddle horn with a clenched right fist. 'Those backwoods' white trash are thumbing their noses at us, Barker, making us look like fools! We have to take the initiative, and we can't do that until someone, for whatever reason, informs on the rebs. So, do your best with that farmer.'

Barker grinned. 'I'll take Jeb Newton with me, Capt'n. His rough ways will loosen any sodbuster's tongue.'

Snake was too far away to hear what was passing between the captain and the thickset red leg. When he and another red leg mounted up and rode south,

114

Snake knew immediately where the pair were heading for. Betty Anne's pa's farm. Knowing the rep of the red legs it smelt like big trouble for Mr Lawson if they found out he had been sheltering the men who helped to kill three of their buddies.

Then Snake had to make a quick decision. Should he stay here on watch until all the red legs moved out and report back to Luther in which direction they had gone, as he had been ordered to do? Or trail the two red legs to the Lawson farm and help them out if things turned nasty for them. The wellbeing of Betty Anne won out. But Snake hoped to hell Luther would see it his way when he had to explain later the reason why he didn't do what he had been told to do. First though, he had to get by the two red-leg look-outs on the crest. He grinned, he was part Indian, wasn't he? It should be natural to him to work his way by two white-eyes who weren't looking down at their feet but were scanning the flats below.

Through the glasses Luther saw that the red-leg patrol was breaking up then he caught the glimpse of the trail dust of riders coming his way. He slid to the bottom of the ditch and swung on to his saddle, but lay low down across his horse's neck. His hands gripped the reins tight and his heels were poised ready to dig hard into his mount's ribs for a mad-ass gallop to safety. He had panicked for nothing. The red legs, five of them, rode passed him at a gentle canter, chatting amongst each other. They didn't know that four rebs were within gunshot range of them. He hoped that the Missourians lying low in the timber would let them pass by, he wasn't ready to start the war yet.

Muttering a thankful prayer, Luther dismounted and climbed back on to the rim once more to wait for Snake to show up and tell him where the rest of the red legs had ridden off to. After a half-hour of an impatient vigil he scanned the ridge and the rock fall with his glasses once more, and saw no sign of any movement. He began to have the worrying thought that Snake had run into big trouble. He'd heard no sounds of gunfire, but that didn't mean that the red legs hadn't grabbed hold of the kid. He could be a prisoner with the captain's bunch, destined to be strung up on the handiest tree. Luther felt it was time to discuss what to do next regarding the disappearance of Snake, and the tactics in their fight against the red legs, with the Missourians. He climbed back on to his horse, pushed the Winchester into its boot and rode along the trail to the Missourians hole-up.

Dismounting in the timber, Luther wasted no time relating to the three rebs about Snake not returning from his scouting. 'I don't know if the kid is still alive, or hangin' from some cottonwood,' he said gloomily. 'Or where the red legs he was going to watch are making for. We're back were we started, the red legs running loose, only we've lost one of our men. What do you boys think our next move should be? To pick up the trail of the red legs the captain's leading, hoping that Snake is still alive and we can somehow effect his rescue? I haven't any other ideas.'

'You're not thinkin' straight, Luther,' Billy said. 'What that capt'n has done is to split up his outfit and send them out seekin' information about us fellas. He's doin' it military style by quarterin' the territory. Those

116

five red legs that passed by here not so long ago were headin' north, some will be headin' west—'

'And the captain must have sent men to the nearest farm to the landslip,' interrupted Luther, his face lighting up. 'And Snake, who, in spite of being part Indian and an owlhoot killer to boot, got kindly treated by a pretty white girl. Such-like friendliness he would never have had before. He's bound to feel beholden to the girl and I'll bet the young hellion is trailing whoever the captain has despatched to the farm to try and prevent any harm coming to the girl or her parents. And I figure he could do with some help. OK, boys, mount up and let's renew our acquaintance with the Lawsons!'

'Jeb', Barker said, pulling up his mount on the rise above the house and barns, 'farmers bend their backs on their growin' land from sun-up to sun-down so that fella down there must have seen men, strangers to him, ridin' along this trail within the last few days or so.' He hard-eyed Jeb. 'M'be more than just seen, Jeb. So we'll snoop around his property to see if we can spot any signs of where men have made camp before we ride down and have words with him.'

They moved away from each other and, slow riding their horses along the edge of the planted land, leaned over their saddles and hawk-eyed the ground for tracks made by horses with men on their backs.

'I've found something, Earl!' Jeb shouted.

Barker rode over to a triumphantly grinning Jeb who was standing beside the dark, narrow mouth of a cave entrance almost hidden by an overgrown tangle of brush and grass. He was waving a strip of cloth.

'Bloodstained,' he said. 'And there's a stove inside, and blankets. At least three, four rebs have been livin' in there, and one of them with a gunshot wound. They could be part of the bunch we sent scatterin' a week or so back. Poor Denny reckoned he'd put a shell in one of them. That bastard sodbuster has been shelterin' them.'

Barker wolf-grinned. 'I'll tell him that's the reason we're takin' him to Plattsville to be strung up and his shack's goin' to get burned down.'

Jethro was working in the hay barn when he heard the click of a pistol being cocked behind him. Blood chilling, he swung round in alarm and faced two men standing framed in the doorway. It didn't have to be written down who they were, and that they knew he had been harbouring reb fugitives. Their cold-grinning faces told him that. Jethro cursed himself for not making sure the cave had been cleaned out after the rebs had left.

It was the bigger of the two red legs who told him his fate. 'We've found where some rebs have been hidin' out, pilgrim. You've just booked yourself a rope on the hangin' tree at Plattsville. My captain will personally slip the noose round your neck.'

'I'll go across to the shack, Earl,' Jeb said, 'and clear out this sodbuster's family before I put the place to the torch.'

'Yeah, you do that,' replied Barker. 'I'll tie this fella up then we can get him a horse for the ride to his hangin'.'

Jethro groaned and his shoulders sagged as Jeb walked out of the barn. He felt as though he was already dead. His Good Samaritan act had destroyed not only his own life but Cassie's and Betty Anne's as well. It was no good appealing to the fat-gutted red leg not to burn down his home; those sons-of-bitches, he knew, were as lacking in mercy as a bronco Apache out on a killing spree. He did have a fleeting, wild-ass thought of plunging the hayfork into the red-leg's guts and then grabbing hold of his rifle and running to the house and putting paid to his partner before he caught on that things had gone wrong for them. Cold reason told him that would only get him killed in front of his family – something he wouldn't want them to see. Dejectedly, he dropped the fork to the ground.

Snake was laid flat behind the stock watering tank, his aching feet and his tiredness forgotten as he saw Mr Lawson, with his hands tied behind his back, being led out of the barn by one of the red legs. A terrified looking Mrs Lawson and Betty Anne, arms clutching each other, were standing on the porch, watched over by the other red leg.

He had been lucky to have slipped past the red-leg look-outs on the ridge. While he was trying to work out if it was worth the risk to scramble up the last few feet of the gully, then leave its cover to try and creep over the crest without the alarm being raised, he heard a shout from below him of 'We've found Wilson's body, Capt'n!' On hearing that call, the look-out men came off the ridge and walked past him to watch the body being dragged out from under the rocks. In a blur of movement Snake was out of the gully and rolling over the rimline and running along the reverse slope the way he had come to start the landslip.

Once he was well clear of the red legs he crossed over to the trail side of the ridge. Then, foot-slipping and ass-sliding down the slope, he reached the trail and started running in earnest. When the trail twisted he dropped down on to the bottom lands, trying to run as arrow-shot straight as possible to the farm, heedless of the pain his tight riding boots were causing him.

All the while as the sweat poured off him, making it difficult to hold on to his rifle, he thought of what the red legs could do to Betty Anne, a white girl who had spoken friendly to him, a 'breed killer. Honour, Indian or white, had to be upheld.

And now here he was, wondering how he could pay off that debt he owed her, and her ma and pa.

Snake thought about stepping out into the open so he could get a clear shot at the two red legs, but they were men more experienced than he was at shoot-outs. He had no doubt that he could down one of them but the red leg still up on his feet would kill him for sure and all the pain and sweat would have been for nothing, unless he could get ahead of them on the trail when they were taking Mr Lawson to wherever they were going to hang him and bushwhack the sons-of-bitches. He set himself to make a dash to cut back on to the Lodge Pole trail when he heard the red leg on the house porch say, 'Just hang on a tad, Earl. I ain't had the pleasure of a purty girl since I don't know when. Then I'll put torch to this shack.'

Snake saw the leering man grab Betty Anne by the waist and haul her, kicking wildly and screaming, into the house. Mrs Lawson rushed, arms flailing, at her daughter's attacker in a frantic attempt to pull her away from him. The red leg knocked her to the ground with a vicious backhanded blow with his fist.

'You bastards, leave her alone!' Jethro sobbed. 'You've got me, ain't that enough?'

Barker grinned at the wild-eyed, madly struggling Jethro. 'It ain't no good gettin' yourself all worked up, sodbuster. You oughta have known that consortin' with rebs would bring a whole heap of trouble on you and your kin.' His grin widened. 'And it won't comfort you none by tellin' you that Jeb will be gentle with your fine-lookin' girl.'

Jethro could only stand sobbing and cursing the red legs.

The rage inside Snake flared white hot. He had never felt a killing blood lust before. The killing of the red legs had to take place here, and fast. It took all his control not to yank out his knife and run across to the shack whooping like a full blood Indian, banking on surprise to allow him to get inside and slice open the bastard's throat who was having his way with Betty Anne. Instead, keeping low, he made for the rear of the shack, grimly promising himself that within the next few minutes he would be giving out two death cries. Silently though, so as not to scare Betty Anne more than she must be right now.

Betty Anne, almost sick with fear, still fought with all her strength to break free from her attacker and the fearful things he was going to do to her. She could smell his rank body sweat, feel the bristle stubble on his unshaven cheeks as he pressed his face to hers to kiss her on the mouth. His hand reached down and snapped the waistband of her skirt and tore the garment from her body. Betty Anne gave a despairing cry as she felt the hot stickiness of the red leg's hand on her naked thigh.

Suddenly she heard him give a deep sighing moan and his hands loosened their terrifying hold on her. Then he seem to have lost the use of his legs and fell away from her and slumped to the floor. Only then did Betty Anne see Snake with the big knife in his hand. A Snake with such a fearsome look on his face she wondered if it was the same boy she had spoken to in the barn. The next thing she knew she was in his arms sobbing loudly her relief.

Snake gently eased her away from him. 'You're OK now, Betty Anne,' he told her soothingly. He toed the dead red leg. 'He won't hurt you any more. Now get down on to the floor and stay there till I deal with his pard. There could be some wild shots comin' this way.'

Snake could have picked off the red leg from the safety of the shack, but his killing lust was still running wild. His pride demanded that he had to meet at least one of his enemies face to face so he would know who had killed him, in the last few seconds he had left to live after he'd had six Colt shells fired into his hide.

Glancing out of a window, he saw the red leg coming up to the house. Mr Lawson, sitting roped up on a horse, would be well out of his line of fire. He turned and gave Betty Anne a warning frown to stay put, then, pushing the knife back into his belt, he drew his pistol and cocked it.

Barker was thinking that he could spare some time to enjoy the young girl once Jeb had done with her; the sodbuster was securely trussed up. His pleasant thoughts were shattered as hell in the shape of a pistol firing boy burst out of the shack. Barker had no time to do anything but die.

Snake's first two shots, fired before he had cleared the porch, ripped their deadly way through Barker's chest, fixing for eternity his shocked surprised look. The third and fourth shells caused high body wounds which spun him around as though buffeted by a high wind before collapsing face down to the ground. Snake's last shot was fired at point blank range while standing over Barker.

Snake stood there for a few seconds looking at the body. It had been a good killing and his Indian blood began to cool down. He reloaded his pistol as quickly as his trembling fingers could slip the shells into the chamber and slipped it back into its holster. Then he ran across to Jethro.

'Is Betty Anne all right, Snake?' an anxious-faced Jethro asked. 'Has she been used by that bastard?'

'She's OK, Mr Lawson,' replied Snake as he cut Jethro's bounds. 'She'll be a mite shook up that's all, I knifed the sonuvabitch before he could do her any harm.'

Jethro dismounted and gripped Snake's shoulders. 'Snake,' he said, his eyes moist, 'the Lawson family will be beholden to you for the rest of our lives.' Jethro managed a weak grin. 'If any lawman is pressin' you too hard you know where there's a handy hole-up and where you'll not be short of good home-cooked chow. Now I'd better check on Ma, that red leg you knifed dealt her a hard blow.'

Snake followed Jethro up to the house, feeling that

in a couple of days or so he had made some good friends, a pleasant relationship he had never experienced before. As they got to the porch, a white-faced Betty Anne came out of the house and ran along to her mother. She knelt down at her side and cradled her head in her arms. 'Ma's coming to, Pa,' she said. 'Are you both OK?' She cast a frightened look at the dead red leg.

'I'm all right, Betty Anne,' Snake said.

'We're all OK thanks to Snake here,' Jethro said. He glanced at Snake. 'I can't keep callin' you Snake, boy, it's kinda undignified. What is your real name?'

'Purcell, Whitney Purcell, Mr Lawson,' replied Snake.

'Whitney.' Jethro reflected for a moment. 'That's a fine name.' His grin this time was deeper. 'Though takin' in account what's just happened here, Snake is the more fittin' name.'

Snake's grin was cut off on hearing Betty Anne's cry of, 'Riders coming in, Pa!'

Snake cursed silently as he grabbed for his pistol and spun round. He wasn't roused up enough to have another shoot-out. Then he stayed his hand with a deep sigh of relief. 'It's OK, it's the marshal and the three Missourians!'

THIRTEEN

Luther drew up his horse at the house, noting the body lying in front of it. The Missourians stayed well back, rifle butts resting on saddles, ready for quick action. They were men, Snake thought, who took nothing on chance and calmly prepared for the worst. He grinned inwardly. And he had gone into a killing situation as heavy-footed as a charging buffalo. But the Missourians hadn't witnessed what the red leg was doing to Betty Anne.

Luther gave Snake an enquiring look. 'Is what you came here for over?'

'Yeah,' Snake replied. 'There's another dead one inside.' He bold-eyed Luther. 'I know I should have stayed at the landslip until the captain had moved out with the rest of his men, Luther, then gone back to tell you which direction they were headin' in. But when I figured where these two bastards were ridin' to I had—'

'Luther,' Jethro butted in, 'If Whitney hadn't showed up when he did my daughter would have been raped. And I would have been on my way to Plattsville to be strung up for helpin' out those three boys back there.'

Luther straightened up in his saddle. 'Plattsville, you said, Jethro?'

Jethro pointed to the dead red leg. 'That's what that bastard told me. And how his captain would enjoy puttin' the noose round my neck.'

'Plattsville's some ten miles west of here, Luther,' Snake said.

Luther favoured Whitney with a congratulatory nod. 'You did right to come here, Snake. As well as saving Betty Anne from being used you lowered the odds against us by two guns.' He waved for the Missourians to come on in. 'It's OK, boys, our help isn't needed, Snake's sorted things out. And got himself a horse. Plus we know where the captain and his vigilantes are.'

The Missourians had dumped the bodies in the Lodge Pole and watched them twisting and turning until they disappeared from their sight, well downstream of Jethro's land.

Jethro and his family, with their arms clutching each other, were saying their goodbyes to Luther and his men. To ride out and do some more killing, Jethro thought. Or to be killed. Though somehow he didn't think that would happen. Not to these men. All signs of the killings had been cleared up, only the frightening memories of how worse things could have been remained. Jethro pulled Betty Anne closer to him.

Betty Anne couldn't hold back her tears. She knew she would never see Snake again. Even if he had been a white boy she would never have been able to have a closer girl-boy relationship. Snake was, she had to admit, a boy who lived by the gun and would, before he got much older, die by the gun. The tears flooded down her cheeks. She would try and remember him as the quick smiling boy she had fed in the barn, and who saved her from a fearful fate.

The five of them were mounted up and had said their last farewells. 'Jethro,' Chuck said, 'you and your family have had some bad trouble because of us, but not any more. I give you my word that no red leg will ever step on your land again, isn't that so, boys?'

'Not unless they can climb out of the six-foot holes on some Boot Hill and ride here,' Billy said flatly.

'Do you believe what Billy said, Jethro?' Mrs Lawson asked, as the dust of the five riders was lost from sight.

'Ma,' replied Jethro, 'if you had seen young Whitney deal with those two red legs you'd have no doubts at all. That bunch of red legs' huntin' days are over.'

Once clear of the farm, Luther called out for Snake to ride up alongside him.

'Snake,' he said, 'if that one-eyed captain's working out of Plattsville it figures that the five red legs who rode past me, and the Missourians must have to swing south once they've finished their scouting to report back to the captain. Now I'm banking on you, boy, to know where the trail they'll use lies. And familiar enough with it to show me a spot where we could be sitting waiting for them with all the edge in our favour.'

Snake grinned. 'I can take you to the Plattsville trail

but you, once bein' a captain, will have to pick your own killin' ground.'

'Fair enough,' said an equally grinning Luther. 'Now get up ahead and ride point.'

FOURTEEN

'Palmer and Webster are ridin' in, Chenney!' Dexter, who was on watch, called out.

Chenney got up from the fire still holding his mug of coffee. 'They ain't rushin' in, Dexter,' he grunted. 'So it looks as though they've had the same stinkin' luck as we've had tryin' to find some fella who'll point us in the direction of some reb sonsuvbitches.'

The five red legs had split up to speed up their search for the information the captain so urgently needed. Palmer and Webster riding north to the Butterfield stage post close to the Kansas border, Chenney with Dexter and Renwick taking in the small farms and holdings west of the trail. Both groups to meet at Bear Creek crossing.

'Any luck, boys?' Chenney asked Palmer, as both men pulled up their mounts at the camp-fire.

Palmer, leaning across his saddle horn, shook his head. 'Naw. Either there ain't any rebs hereabouts, or they've got wind of us and are lyin' real low someplace. Though it could be the fellas me and Webster questioned have been lyin' their heads off to us.'

'Could be, Palmer, could well be,' replied Chenney. 'Though the captain believes that the rebs who killed our boys at the landslip are still close by and are only waitin' to jump us again. Step down, boys, and have some coffee, then we'll head back to Plattsville to see how the captain's made out.'

Within twenty minutes the red legs had broken camp and were up on their horses and riding south-west to rendezvous with their captain. Five miles on, Dexter raised his hand and the trio halted. 'There's smoke showin' above that tree-line, Chenney,' he said. 'Enough of it to be comin' from some dirt farmer's shack's chimney.'

'It's worth payin' it a visit,' Chenney said. 'If you're right, Dexter, the shack could be used as a reb hole-up. It's a likely spot for them, well away from any main trail.' He grinned. 'M'be we'll get lucky.'

They drew up their mounts on the steep rise move the ramshackle cabin and the equally broken-down barn. A narrow creek ran between the two buildings and twenty or so longhorns were chewing at the grass on both sides of the water.

'There's only a coupla horses in that corral,' Chenney said. 'So I guess that cabin ain't occupied by a bunch of rebs. Ride down there, Webster, and ask the owner if he's seen any rebs hereabouts. More than likely it will be a waste of time, but the captain said we had to check on every spread, farm or whatever, in this section.'

Ben Bradley, the owner of the shack and the herd of cows until he had changed their brands and sold them on to a rancher who wasn't too fussy seeing bills of sale,

130

was crouched down at a window with a double-barrelled shotgun in his hands, eyeing suspiciously the riders on the ridge.

'Are those bastards a sheriff's posse, Pa?' Saul, his son, asked.

'Could well be, son,' replied Bradley, not taking his gaze off the riders. 'Could be some of that ranch's crew we lifted those cows from. Whoever they are they've sure gone outa their way to pay us a call.' He gave a gap-toothed smile. 'Could be a bunch of no-good cattle-thieves reckonin' on liftin' our cows.'

'One of them's comin' down, Pa,' Saul said.

'It ain't likely he's about to knock on our door askin' for directions on account of him and his buddies have got themselves lost on the wild prairie,' his pa replied. 'But him comin' in on his ownsome could work to our advantage, boy. Whoever they are up there it means trouble for us, I can smell it. And too big for us to fight off. So it's quittin' time. As soon as I blow that fella to kingdom come we'll make a bolt for our horses. The blastin' of him should have those fellas on the ridge wonderin' what to do next for a coupla minutes or so, long enough for us to make it to the corral.' Ben grinned at his son. 'Though it'll mean ridin' the mounts the way those bare-assed red devils favour 'cos we ain't got the time to throw saddles across their backs.'

Webster dismounted and stepped up to the shack. He knew someone was inside as he could hear them moving about, and reached out a hand to knock on the door. Before he could do so the door creaked part open and he glimpsed a scowling bearded-faced man, and the shotgun he held pointing at him. The shotgun roared and flamed and a bloody, chest-shattered, dead Webster was hurled back from the door several yards, landing on the ground with a dust-raising thud at his horse's feet.

Ben and his son cleared the shack in a low-backed weaving run. They just about made it to the corral when Saul felt a searing blow in the small of his back that sent him stumbling forward a few more paces on legs that didn't seem to belong to him. He gave out a strangled cry of, 'Pa, I'm kilt!'

Ben whirled round as he was scrambling under the corral fencing in time to see his son drop to the ground. Then a barrage of Winchester shells kicked up the dirt all around him forcing him to shelter behind a thick fence post. He cursed. So much for catching the sons-of-bitches by surprise. He had got his boy shot down like a mad dog and they had him pinned down with only a short-range scatter-gun and a pistol to defend himself with.

Ben risked a look round the post and saw that only two men were firing at him from the ridge, the other two must be working their way around him. And he also found out that the man he had killed wasn't some town hanger-on earning himself some drinking money by being deputized to join a sheriff's posse but, by his boots, a red leg. That set him off in another bout of cursing, more profound this time. No wonder he hadn't been able to win some time for him and his boy to reach the corral unharmed, by shooting his unwanted visitor.

The red-legs' fast killing rep was well known and his

foolish act by killing one of their kind had got their dander up. Why they should have showed up outside his shack had him foxed. One thing was for sure, Brad thought bitterly, he had got his boy shot and he himself was about to go the same way.

In a slight pause in the gunfire Ben heard the clink of metal against metal behind an old plough several yards away to his left. He twisted round and pulled off the second load in the shotgun beneath the plough and had the satisfaction of hearing a howl of pain and a shout of 'The old bastard's peppered me, Palmer! Get round him for Chris'sake!'

'You're lucky, friend,' Ben muttered, 'the next time I won't miss; I want an eye for an eye, one of you bastards for my boy.' He thumbed two reloads into the shotgun and laid his pistol on the ground by his side, ready as ever he would be when the red-legs' patience ran out and they rushed him.

'Did you hear that, Luther?' Snake said. 'Gunfire beyond those trees to our left!'

They were riding along the trail that Snake had told them the red legs would use to reach Plattsville, and where the thick stands of timber, on both sides of the trail, would, in Luther's expert opinion, make that stretch of the trail an ideal killing ground, a red-leg killing ground.

Every so often the Missourians dismounted and read the trail. They had picked up tracks of single riders, two riders, and the wheel marks of a wagon, but had cut no sign of five men riding together.

'They're still ahead of us, Luther,' Billy said, as he

swung back into his saddle.

Luther gave an acknowledging grunt. The red legs may still be ahead of them but he wanted to get his men into an ambush position as soon as he could. He didn't dispute the brush boys reading of the trail that the red legs were still north of them, but for how long was his worry? They could be only a mile or two away and closing in on them fast.

Luther listened for moment or two to the distant firing then turned to face Snake. 'I can hear a shotgun cutting loose, Snake,' he said. 'What's over that hill, a farm, a ranch?'

Snake grinned. 'Naw. It's old Ben Bradley's place over there. That's his shotgun you heard. Him and his son are small-time cattle-thieves. They lift the cattle from some ranch across the line in Kansas, drive them down to his back of the beyond place then, when he's altered the longhorn's brands, so it looks like he's their legal owner, he sells them to any rancher willin' to pay cash on the barrel and asking no questions.'

'If this fella Bradley is a noted cattle-thief, Luther,' Joe said, 'it's more than likely the others who are doin' the shootin' are a sheriff's posse. And yet we know that five red legs are up here someplace askin' questions about our whereabouts and we know that those sonsuvbitches tend to use their guns when askin' questions. It'll pay us to ride over there and check on the fellas who are shootin' at Bradley, Luther.'

Luther did some rapid rethinking of his tactics. Finally he said, 'Me and Snake will go. You boys get settled down in those trees ready for when those red legs come riding into rifle range. All of us don't want to go to see what all the shooting's about, the red legs could slip by us and we may never come across a finer spot to set up an ambush before they reach Plattsville. Though if you're right, Joe, and the shootists are red legs, I'll send the kid haring back for you all, OK?'

'OK, Luther,' Billy said. 'We'll get the ambush set up.' He grinned. 'Three against five ain't bad odds, especially when we've surprise and cover goin' for us.'

Bradley winced and dirty-mouthed as a shell fired from the red leg working his way round him hissed close by his head. Soon, he knew, the son-of-a-bitch would be in a position to pull off a killing back shot, like his boy had taken. It didn't take long for Bradley to sort out his options. He could either stay put and die, or make a wild dash at the red leg, blazing away at him with his shotgun, and die. His choice was to die on his feet fighting back.

Bradley was banking on the red leg who had howled he had been wounded being a little slow in his reactions, gun wise. He didn't reckon that the riflemen on the ridge would be caught off guard; they hadn't been when he and his boy fled the shack. They were a risk he was honour bound to take, being beholden to his dead boy to kill at least one red-feg before he was gunned down.

Bradley drew back both hammers of the shotgun and brought his knees up and, taking a deep breath, sprang to his feet and ran at the man in the gully, screaming a reb yell he hadn't sounded since charging the blue-bellies' lines at Gettysburg.

With a 'What the hell' look on his face, Palmer

couldn't stop himself from raising his head above the edge of the gully on hearing the banshee-like wail. Bradley discharge both barrels on the run. The gun kicked high in his hands and only part of its deadly hail hit Palmer, enough to turn his face into a fearful, dripping, red mash and push him back on to the bed of the ditch.

A Winchester shell caught Bradley in the fleshy part of his right thigh and his leg gave away beneath him, tumbling him headfirst on top of the dead Palmer as more shells cut through the air behind him.

Bradley rolled painfully off the body, feeling the stickiness of blood on his shirt from the mess of a face. He was past being able to move around and could only wait until the riflemen came in real close for their killing shots, and see if he could get in one deadly shot of his own. On the good side he had killed two red legs and wounded a third, and got himself a rifle. He had avenged his boy's death in spades. Bradley managed a grin. If he came through the next few minutes OK he'd gain a rep as a *pistolero*.

Luther and Snake had got as close to the firing up on their horses as they dared risk. Now, on foot after picking their way around the side of the high ground in front of Bradley's property, they had a clear view of the one-sided gun battle taking place below them, and that one of the men Bradley had downed wore red boots.

'Joe was right, Snake,' Luther said. 'Mr Bradley has been set upon by a bunch of red legs and, by the look of it, he's been drawing their blood more than somewhat. One lying dead in front of his shack, another looking likewise stretched out in that ditch where Mr

Bradley's making his stand. And the red leg all curled up this side of that plough seems to have quit the fight.' Luther's face hardened. 'I take it, Snake, that the boy lying beside the corral is Mr Bradley's son.'

'Yeah, that's poor Saul,' replied Snake. 'Him and his pa were real close. No wonder old Ben's got himself worked up into a killin' mood.'

'The two firing from the ridge make five of the bastards,' continued Luther. 'The bunch the Missourians are arranging a surprise party for.'

'Do you want me to ride back to the trail for them, Luther?' Snake asked.

Luther shook his head. 'We haven't got any time to lose if we want to prevent Mr Bradley from ending up like his boy. Those red legs are moving down so they can get a clear shot at him.' Luther studied the lie of the ridge for minute or two then gave Snake his orders.

'You belly down here, Snake,' he said, 'and draw their fire from Mr Bradley. Force them to go to ground and it will give me chance to rush them from where they won't be expecting trouble, behind them. But don't get too excited, stay low. Show an inch of your flesh and those fellas will put a shell in it. OK?' Before Snake could reply he had taken off, back the way they had come on to the high ground.

Snake, taking heed of Luther's warning, dropped to the ground behind a natural barrier of rocks and, pressing his rifle into his shoulder, began firing. The brush was too thick from where the red legs were firing for him see if he had hit one of them, though they ceased firing for a while and when they opened up again it was coming his way, easing Mr Bradley's plight. The shells

137

winged off the rocks, showering him with splinters and forcing him to hug the ground. In spite of that danger-ous discomfort, Snake knew he had the easy part of the action. Luther was going to do the killing and against odds not in his favour. He raised himself up, aimed his rifle, and pulled off shots as fast as he could lever the shells into the chamber.

Suddenly Snake thought of a danger Luther hadn't mentioned: Mr Bradley. If the old man spotted Luther coming over the rim before he started firing at the red legs he would naturally take him for one of the gang and cut loose at him. Somehow he would have to warn Mr Bradley to hold his fire, even if that meant showing more than a couple of inches of his flesh. Snake gave a faint twist of a smile. His chance came when the red-legs' fire ceased, to reload their guns he opined, and he leapt to his feet, waving his rifle above his head to attract Bradley's attention and yelling, 'It's me, Snake! Stop firin'!'

Ben Bradley had been trying to puzzle out who his saviour was drawing the red-leg fire away from him. Not since the war had he worked with men who would have stuck their necks out for him. He had never even had a partner in his cattle-lifting activities, only his dead boy, Saul. He was still puzzled on seeing that the man who had come to his aid was the young 'breed owlhoot, Snake. And the kid's call for him to stop firing had him confused until he cottoned on to the fact that the kid wasn't on his own but must have others with him, and whoever they were, were planning to jump the two red legs. He waved his hand at Snake acknowledging his understanding of the situation, but Snake was already kissing the dirt again as another fusillade of shells tore through the air above him. He hoped Mr Bradley had got the message; he hadn't the balls to stand upright again and offer himself as a target to a couple of expert riflemen. Snake took a grip of himself, Luther was relying on him and he raised himself slightly and once more fired across at the red legs.

Luther paused just below the crest. He had no idea how far down the red legs were, or if he would be able to see them lying there among the thick brush. He had no time to work out any other tactics than hauling himself over the rim line and going down the far side shooting as soon as he had a target. It wasn't a mad-assed, 'Glory boy' plan. Luther knew that even the most hardened gunmen, men like the red legs, tend to become unnerved somewhat on being attacked suddenly from behind them. Unsettled enough, he hoped, for them to show themselves to the rifles of Snake and the old cattle-thief. Luther laid his rifle on the ground and drew both pistols, cocked them, and made his move.

Luck was with him on two counts. As he came over the ridge he immediately saw the red legs, leastways their backs, though a long range pistol shot below him.

The slope was firm beneath his feet so he could move with some haste without having the worry he could lose his balance and slide past the red legs on his ass, unable to use his pistols.

He was twenty feet down the grade and the red legs were still unaware of their danger. Luther was not yet within accurate pistol-killing range, but thought that it was time he unsettled the two ambushers: it would be pushing his streak of good luck to try and get any closer without opening fire. If one of them half turned to reload his rifle he would be seen, and he wanted to be the one who started the shooting, on the old maxim that he who hits first generally hits the hardest. Both men were firing in Snake's direction so their rifle discharges would drown the lighter cracks of his pistol at least until he got several feet nearer. He began firing, in left-gun then right-gun sequence.

Chenney, higher up on the slope than Renwick, had rolled over on to his side to reload his rifle, and saw a wild-faced man bearing down on him, a two-pistol firing man. Alarmed, he gave out an explosive, 'Jesus Christ!', and dropped his rifle and the reloads and grabbed frantically for his pistol as he rose to his knees.

A shell from Luther's left-hand pistol punched another eye in Chenney's face just above the bridge of his nose, a crimson-ringed unseeing eye. Chenney fell over backwards then lay still, legs folded beneath him. Luther didn't give him a second glance as he passed by him, the red leg was dead for real.

Renwick, hearing the shooting behind him, turned and faced his unexpected attacker. He caught a fleeting glimpse of Chenney's body. He cursed, and with the quick reactions of a man who earned his keep by the use of his gun, he snapped off a shot at Luther from a waist-high-held rifle. The shell missed Luther and Renwick never got the time to take another shot. Luther didn't think he had fatally hit the red leg with his nonstop burst of firing, but he saw him drop his rifle and fall face down to the ground as straight and true as a felled tree. Either Snake or the old man's rifle had fired the killing shot. All that mattered was that the red legs were accounted for and he and Snake and Mr Bradley were still breathing. He waved a hand held high to signify to them that it was all over on the ridge, then walked back over the rim to pick up his rifle.

As Snake came down to check on the red leg lying beside the plough, he heard the sound of three spaced rifle shots and guessed that Luther was sending the message to the Missourians to come on in. He looked down at the painfully groaning red leg and saw that the legs of his pants were black with blood from the shot-gun blast and he didn't have to be a doctor to know that the man was no longer a threat to them. Just to make sure Snake kicked the red leg's rifle well clear of him and took his pistol from out of its holster and pushed it into the top of his pants, then he dashed across to help Bradley who was trying to lift his son's body off the ground.

'I'll thank you and your pard, Snake,' Bradley said, 'after I get my boy's body inside and get him cleaned up for his burial. Now I would be more grateful if you could give me a hand; I ain't got the strength to lift him on my own. One of those sonsuvbitches you and your pard dealt with put a slug in my right leg. It's a good clean wound but it still hurts like hell.'

'Here, take my rifle, Mr Bradley,' Snake said, 'I'll do the liftin'.' He handed the Winchester over to the old man. And with some effort he managed to heave Saul's body across his shoulders and carried it to the shack. A heavy limping Bradley followed behind him.

Snake laid the body gently on the cot. 'You do what you have to do, Mr Bradley,' he said. 'I'll dig Saul's grave, if you tell me where you want it digging.'

'There's a small burial plot just out back, Snake,' Bradley replied. 'Ma and Saul's young sister's lyin' there; spades are in the barn. I'll come out and give you a hand as soon as I'm finished here.'

A heavy sweating Snake had dug a hole about three feet deep when Luther showed up at his side. 'Is the old man OK?' he asked.

'He's been shot in the leg, but he can hobble around right,' replied Snake. 'He's inside seein' to his boy. Are you OK?'

Luther thin-grinned. 'Better than those two red legs I left up there. I helped that wounded one on to his horse. He was moaning on about how badly wounded he was. Then I told him that three former Missourian brush boys were coming in at any moment holding a devil's hatred in their hearts against red legs, so, sorely wounded or not, he rode out of here at a fair lick.' He cold-smiled again. 'We've done just fine here, Snake; the Missourians will be as mad as hell at not taking part in the shindig. Give me the spade, while you go and bring in all the horses. I want to waste no time getting back on to the Plattsville trail once the boys ride in.'

All the dead had been buried and Luther and his men were ready to ride on to Plattsville to confront the captain and the three vigilantes he had with him, Luther feeling confident that they had all the edge over the captain.

'We'll be moving out now, Mr Bradley,' he said. 'And, as I've already told you, I'm sorry me and Snake didn't get here in time to save your boy but between us we made them pay a high price for killing him. And there's five less of the sonsuvbitches for me and the boys to face.'

A puzzled Ben Bradley watched them go. He was sure he had seen a marshal's badge pinned on the big Texan's shirt when his duster had flapped open. But would a lawman lead a posse of such roughnecks as the Missourians, and with the wanted killer, Snake, in tow? And would one of Judge Parker's marshals let him, a known cattle-thief, keep the red legs mounts, and all their guns? Bradley shook his head. The upset of the shooting of his son must have made him see things that weren't there. The killing trouble could only be a settlement of old wartime feuds. Bradley almost felt sorry for the red legs in Plattsville; though they didn't know it yet, they were due for an early grave on Boot Hill.

Captain Chartris paced to and fro in his hotel room, chewing savagely on the ragged end of a cigar that had long since gone out, but he was too preoccupied with worrying thoughts to relight it. The lamps were being lit in town and still Barker and Jeb Wallace hadn't returned from their mission to question the farmer whose land lay the closest to the fatal land slip. They should have reported in hours ago. He had to accept the ominous implication that the pair were dead; somehow they had been ambushed by the reb fugitives.

The captain wasn't too worried about the five men he had sent north, yet. They'd had further to travel and could have picked up a lead that had taken them to the Kansas border. But still, he thought, Chenney should have had the wisdom to send one of his men here to appraise him of his intentions. The old saying that no news is good news didn't ease his worries any.

A wave of fear swept over the captain. As a soldier he had experienced fear before, just before a charge at a reb position, which quickly passed when his blood began to rise as, with sabre drawn, yelling and cursing, he led his company against the enemy line. This spasm of fear was different; it was the fear of the unknown, grinding away painfully in the pit of his stomach, and one he couldn't shake off. Was it a dark foretelling of his future? Was he destined to die, not like a soldier, but to suffer the ignominy of being shot in the back from some dark alley or backwoods ambush? The captain stopped his pacing to gaze, eyes unseeing, out of the window, praying that such-like morbid thoughts were not affecting his men as well.

FIFTEEN

'There it is, boys – Plattsville,' Luther said, nodding in the direction of a cluster of buildings several hundred yards ahead of the stand of timber they were sheltering in. 'That red-leg captain will have accepted by now,' he continued, 'that those men he sent to seek us out aren't coming back and that he's got a fight-to-the-death war on his hands and, I reckon, feeling somewhat uncomfortable knowing he's the prey and no longer the hunter.'

Luther twisted round in his saddle and faced Snake and the three Missourians. 'Now, what we've got to ask ourselves is what the captain's next moves are, and how we can counter them. I don't think he'll ride out with his boys and try and track us down; he hasn't the men for that sort of work. He'll want us to become rash with our successes and ride into town to face them where we'll be out in the open and him and his men will be behind walls. He'll judge that we can't stay out on the plains having our balls frozen with cold night camps in case we give our whereabouts away.'

They had made a night camp not wanting to enter Plattsville, to give the red legs, who could be in any of the buildings they could see, the chance to gun them down in the dark. The sun was now almost at its height and still there wasn't much activity going on in the town, not enough to cover them on the approach to the town let alone ride along Main Street without even the town's dogs recognizing that the three, armed-up, wild-looking Missourians were not just passing through but had serious business to be seen to in Plattsville. The red legs would know they were ex-reb irregulars and gun them down.

'Would that captain risk a shoot-out with us in the middle of Main Street, Luther?' Snake asked. 'He would know that if he pulled through the gunfight the sheriff would come down hard on him for disturbing the peace of his town.'

'Snake,' replied Luther. 'That captain, for some twisted reason or other, is a reb hater. He would shoot us down in front of the Pearly Gates to satisfy that hate.'

'Luther,' Chuck said, 'Me and the boys don't give a hoot what the capt'n's figurin' on doin', but when he makes his move we want to be there to stop it. We know it weren't your intent but you and the kid there have been doin' all the blood-lettin' so far in this campaign. We've been more or less taggin' along with you. It's beholden to me, Joe and Billy to shed some blood; one of the bastards winged me! Even if that means us ridin' bold-assed into that burg and callin' out the sonsuvbitches!'

'Shooting down a man wearing the uniform of a US

146

army captain, Chuck,' Luther said. 'will have every blue belly and peace officer in the Nations hunting you down.'

'Before those red legs bodies hit the dirt of Main Street,' Chuck replied. 'we'll be halfway across Kansas, ass-kickin' it for the Missouri border.' He grinned at Luther. 'We'll leave the killin' of the captain to you and Snake.'

'It could be you boys who hit the dirt,' Luther said, sober-voiced.

'Luther,' Chuck said, 'me and the boys have been livin' with death ridin' close by us for more years than we can reckon.' His face steeled over. 'It would be a relief to let the grim reaper catch up with us as long as we can take some of those bastards down to hell along-side us!'

Luther gave an understanding nod. 'I see your point, boys,' he said. 'But let me and Snake ride into town first to see if we can find out just where they're holed-up then we can come back here and work out a plan. We don't want to give that captain any advantage by going off at half-cock.' He beady-eyed Snake. 'You haven't upset the Plattsville marshal, have you? Enough to haul you off your horse and throw you in his jail if he claps eyes on you?'

'If you mean have I robbed the bank there, well I ain't,' replied Snake. 'Though he could have my like-ness pinned on his office walls.' He grinned. 'But there ain't no need for you to worry, Luther, it won't be a fair likeness.'

'OK then,' Luther said. 'Let's do some scouting.' And he kneed his horse forward with a call over his shoulders that he would see the Missourians in an hour or so.

'That's the first of them, Luther,' Snake said softly.

'I see him,' Luther replied, casually glancing up at the rifleman sitting on the balcony of the first building, a land agent's office, at the beginning of Main Street, Luther knew he had been right to have reined in the Missourians. They wouldn't have made it this far without raising the alarm.

'We'll pull up outside that store, Snake,' he said. 'And make as though I've ridden in for supplies. You stroll across to the saloon and look at any high building at the far end of the street for the other red leg. The captain's bound to have placed look-outs watching both trails into the town.'

'Ain't you wearin' your badge, Luther?' Snake asked. 'Then you could walk openly around the town.'

'If I wore my badge,' Luther said, 'some of the towns-folk would see it and would expect me to call on their sheriff to see if he's holding any prisoners in his jail due to appear in front of Judge Parker. And a trip to Fort Smith right now won't help us in our campaign.'

After a sleepless night, Captain Chartris was still plagued by his fears and doubts. He had prepared as well as he could with the small force he commanded against a sudden attack by an unknown number of reb renegades. He had placed men at both ends of Main Street that gave them a clear view of all the normal trails leading into town while he and the third man, Bilby, patrolled the empty back lots as a precaution against the rebs trying to infiltrate into Plattsville unseen.

'Will the bastards come in, Capt'n?' Bilby asked, after

they had finished the first circuit of the town.

'Oh, they'll ride in all right, Bilby!' the captain said, his good eye flashing angrily. 'The scum slipped through our fingers when we thought we had them boxed in and now they think they have broken us, but, by thunder, they'll find out how wrong they are! They have given us a bloody nose, Bilby, that can't be denied, but it's the winning of the last battle that decides the outcome of a war. And I intend to win it!'

'There's Jackson comin' through that side alley, Capt'n,' Bilby said.

'Have you seen the rebs, Jackson?' the captain called out, as Jackson came towards them across the overgrown wasteland at the rear of the only saloon in Plattsville. 'Could you make out how many of them there are?'

Jackson stopped in front of the captain and, out of long habit, gave him a military salute. 'I ain't seen any rebs, or any other bunch of riders comin' in,' he said. 'But I thought I oughta come and tell you about the tall fella and the 'breed kid who've ridden into town.'

'You haven't left your post just to tell me that two men have come into town?' the captain said icily.

'Hear me out, Capt'n,' a ruffled-tempered Jackson replied. 'I was with Sergeant Barker when we chased after that 'breed who tried to lift one of the army post's horses. We caught up with him at the camp of the big fella I've just seen. The 'breed was all roped up ready for the trip to Judge Parker's court at Fort Smith. The fella told us he was a state marshal, showed us his badge. Now the pair of them have come ridin' in as if they're long time pards, and they're a long way from Fort Smith.'

149

'Both of them could be horse-thieves, Jackson, using a marshal's badge as a subterfuge,' the captain replied.

'They sure didn't look like buddies when I saw them, Capt'n,' Jackson said. 'The big marshal looked mad enough at the 'breed to have put a slug in him.'

Though Captain Chatris didn't think that Jackson's report had any significance, for curiosity's sake he would check on the two mystery riders. Then he thought that he would be chasing shadows if the rebs didn't show their hands soon. 'Where are these two now, Jackson?' he asked.

'The marshal fella is in the general stores, Capt'n,' Jackson said. 'I've lost sight of the 'breed kid.'

The three of them walked back through the alley until they had an unobstructed view of the store yet still in cover, just in time to see Jackson's 'big fella' step out of the store.

The captain stiffened suddenly. He was certain he had seen that hawk face before. Then he remembered: in the saloon at Tampas where he'd briefed his men about the rebs at Willow Creek. And how he had been told that a rider, coming from the direction of Tampas had warned the rebs of their danger. Then Jackson relating that he had seen him close to their camp at the army post, and the killing landslip. Now the 'marshal' had shown up here in Plattsville. Coincidental? The captain wasn't thinking so; he was beginning to see a ominous pattern emerging. Suddenly Jackson's report was highly revelant. What relationship the marshal had with a noted horse-thief he couldn't work out. But a man wearing a marshal's badge could more or less rub shoulders with his men and not be suspected of being a reb sympathizer, and move freely around the territory to warn any reb that his men were closing in on them. The only way he could prove if his reasoning was right was to have a talk with the 'marshal', with or without his consent.

'We are going to question the big man,' he said, 'about how his travels across the territory seem to link with our movements.' The captain smiled. 'Not too harshly though. We do not want to be seen to have no respect for the men who uphold the law in the Nations.' The captain's face stoned over. 'If we find out that he is a spy for the rebs, then naturally we'll shoot him.'

'What about his 'breed pard, Capt'n?' Jackson said.

'He is of no consequence,' replied the captain. 'But when you get back to your post if you see him on the street, shoot him. He is a horse-thief, isn't he? Bilby, let's make our acquantance with the "marshal".'

Luther turned and saw the captain and one of his men crossing the street towards him. He also saw another red leg hurrying along the street. Though he was somewhat tensed up he kept an open, bland expression on his face. There was no need to worry, he told himself, the pair were only crossing the street. And, after all, he had all the authority of Judge Parker backing him up. Then it was too late to worry as the pair instead of passing closed in on either side of him and he felt the sharp prick of a knife point in the small of his back.

'You and I, Marshal,' the captain said, 'are going to have a fruitful talk. Now I want it to be a civilized conversation, but if you're contemplating otherwise,

Mr Bilby has orders to slip that knife between your ribs. Right, let's move, "Marshal".'

The fanatical-eyed glare the captain was giving him, and another painful dig in his flesh from Mr Bilby's knife told Luther that he had no other option, if he wanted to stay alive, but to obey the captain's orders and move. He hoped that Snake would not come mad-ass dashing in to try and rescue him and get them both killed, but use his brains and get back to the Missourians and tell them of how his plan had gone all to hell.

Snake had seen all that had gone on from behind the saloon door. Somehow things had gone wrong for Luther and it was too big for him to put right. It needed the fire power and skills of veteran gunmen, the Missourians. Snake risked a quick look over the swing doors and noticed that the red leg who had passed the saloon was well along the street and figured he was the look-out on the balcony. He stepped quickly outside the saloon and followed in his wake. When the red leg entered the building he would run across the street and make for the camp in the trees. It was too risky to unhitch his horse when the red leg captain and one of his men were standing just across from the saloon. He shot a nervous glance back and saw Luther being bundled into a building at the far end of the street; looking ahead of him again the red leg he was trailing had vanished.

A worried Snake stopped to do some rapid thinking. The man hadn't had time to make it to his look-out post so he must have suspected he was being tailed and ducked into the alley up ahead all set to jump him.

Snake began walking again, slower, tensed-nerved and with his pistol half clear of its holster. Reaching the end of the block he halted once more and leaned forward. Dry-mouthed, with pistol fisted, he peered into the alley – and found himself eyeballing a widely grinning Chuck. 'Holy Moses!' he gasped. 'I was all worked up to have a shoot-out with a goddamned red leg, Chuck!'

A still grinning Chuck jerked a thumb over his shoulder. 'Do you mean that fella, Snake?' Snake looked beyond Chuck and saw Joe dragging a body behind a pile of broken crates. 'We saw you trailin' him while we were waitin' here to greet him when he came back to his post.'

'I was tryin' to make it back to you boys,' Snake said, 'to tell you that Luther's been taken by the captain.'

'We already know that,' Chuck said hard-voiced. 'We're fixin' to rescue him.'

'I thought that Luther told you to stay put in the trees, Chuck?' Snake said.

'Well we weren't too happy at bein' left behind,' Chuck said. 'So when this string of horses came by, driven, accordin' to the drovers, to some ranch on the far side of Plattsville, we took it in our heads to come into town and give you and Luther some back-up if you hit trouble. We came in in your pa's style, under the dust and tails of fast-movin' horses. Then we lay low in a dry wash wonderin' how we could get by that fella I knifed when he obliged us by comin' down and walking along the street. A while later we saw Luther bein' taken. So somehow that one-eyed captain must have found out that he's been helpin' us rebs. It's as well we showed up in town, Snake.'

153

'Have you come up with a plan to rescue Luther?' Snake said.

It was Joe who had joined them who answered. 'Yeah, we've got a plan. We go along to that buildin' where they're holdin' Luther and go in and shoot the bastards dead. Then get to hell outa here, fast.'

Snake thought that Joe was ribbing him but he saw no signs of humour on either of their faces. He was definitely riding with the hard men now. 'Where's Billy?' he asked.

'He's workin' his way to the other end of town,' Chuck said, 'tryin' to find where the other look-out man that captain must have posted is. We need him to be put out of business before we can pay that call on the captain.'

Luther sat on the only chair in what he took to be an abandoned store. The red leg had exchanged his knife for a pistol, held fully cocked only feet away from his head. His badge and Snake's warrant paper had been taken from him and were being looked at by the captain. He had thought that the captain had a look of madness about him, but seeing his drawn, nerve-twiching face, he knew for sure he was loco. The captain must have suspicions that he was working with the rebs. How deep those suspicions were would decide how long he had to live. It was time he played his marshal's card, to the full.

'What the hell are you holding me, a US marshal, at gunpoint for, Captain?' he said angrily. 'Are you passing yourself off as an army captain so you and your boys can rob the bank? Shoot me and Judge Parker will set up

154

one mighty big hunt for you and your gang, a dead or alive hunt!'

Captain Chartris almost physically recoiled at being called a bank robber. He classed himself as a law-abiding man. It had been within the law to hunt down and hang reb renegades, until Washington had decreed otherwise. Though to his way of thinking the rebs were beyond the sanctuary of any law, especially the one John Brown had adhered to, that of an eye for an eye.

'We are not lawbreakers, Marshal,' he replied as angry-voiced as his accuser had been. 'We are tracking down one-time reb irregulars, wanted by the government for crimes committed during the war. It is not an easy task as the secessionist rabble have many sympathizers here in the Nations who give them food and shelter, and intelligence regarding the movements of my command.' His single eye gazed long and hard at Luther. 'I saw you in that saloon in Tampas; some of my men saw you with a prisoner near the Lodge Pole river. After the Tampas sighting, three rebs escaped capture, warned by a rider from Tampas. Then I lost three men in a ambush along the Lodge Pole trail where you had made camp. Now it all could be coincidental, after all you are a marshal and your jurisdiction covers a lot of territory. But if my look-outs spot armed men riding into Plattesville then I can only conclude that you are acting as a scout for the rebs, and will shoot you!' Again came that beady-eyed glare. 'If not, then I'll owe you an apology. In wartime many innocent people get hurt or are wrongly accused of consorting with the enemy.'

Wartime, Enemy! Luther silently gasped. What pain and mental torture had the captain suffered during the

THE JAYHAWKERS

war to not accept it had ended? His ace card had failed. He couldn't expect Snake to get him out of this hole – and he had told the Missourians to stay put in the timber. All he could do was to bold-eye the captain.

'Snake,' Chuck said. 'Me and Joe are goin' to Injun along the street and meet up with Billy and look-out or not we're goin' to get Luther outa that buildin'. No offence to you, kid, but from here on in, it's our business.' He grinned. 'You can go back to your owlhoot ways, but if you still feel obliged to help us you can bring the horses up to the back of that buildin' as soon as the firin' starts up. Whoever of us makes it back through that door still on their feet will need his horse to get a long ways from Plattsville fast.'

Snake knew that there was no time to argue with Chuck that he should go with them. Every minute Luther was in that shack the closer he was to being killed.

'You'll get your horses,' he said. 'And you wild boys take care.'

Spenser, the second look-out's bursting into the room drew the captain's soul-searching gaze from Luther. Angry-faced, he asked why he had left his post.

'I've not only left my post, Capt'n,' replied Spenser, 'but I've quit this doomed outfit!' He looked at Bilby. 'And so would you if you had any sense! Those bastard rebs are in Plattsville and they're wantin' our blood. If we don't get to hell outa this town we'll end up like the rest of the boys, dead!'

'Nonsense!' the captain barked. 'Have you seen any rebs on the street, Spenser?'

156

In spite of his confident statement Luther saw a flash of the same fear that Spenser was giving out, shadow the captain's face. He sat a little more relaxed. The Missourians were on the hunt. All was not lost; unless the crazy captain took it in his mind to shoot him out of hand.

'No I ain't, Capt'n,' Spenser said. 'But put that question to Jackson, if he ain't lyin' dead in some side alley. I ain't seen him since he spoke to you on the street. And wherever he is he ain't at his post! Bilby, if you think that you and the capt'n can hold off God knows how many brush boys then you're crazier than the capt'n.' Spenser turned his back on the captain and walked to the door.

Luther heard the captain give out a howl-like cry then the sound of a pistol discharge echoed in the room. Spenser, without even a groan, fell forward on to his face.

The deadly suddenness of the captain's action shook not only Luther but Bilby as well. Shock-faced his pistol swung away from Luther, though of no advantage to Luther's hopes of escaping. He now had the pistol of a man who had cracked-up pointing at him. In spite of that threat he had to say his piece.

'You said you weren't a law-breaker, Captain,' he said. 'But I reckon that shooting a man in the back, one of your own at that, must overstep the law in any man's view. Judge Parker, across there at Fort Smith, would see it no other way. And it isn't as though the war's still going on and you shot him for cowardice in the face of the enemy.'

'General Grant should never have signed a peace

treaty with you rebs,' a devil-faced captain ranted. 'He should have brought you all down to you knees! I and my men are only doing what he should have carried out. Spenser was a willing party to that and he left his post in face of the enemy! Now I will keep my promise to kill you if the rebs showed up here, though I won't have the pleasure of hanging you!' Saliva flecked his mouth as he brought his pistol to bear on Luther.

Luther braced himself for the painful, killing impact. The shot he heard left him alive and had been fired by Bilby. It had the captain staggering back a few paces with his left hand across his chest watching the blood trickling through his fingers. The captain's expression changed from a mask of wild hatred to one of puzzlement. He gave Bilby a brief, disbelieving look then slowly dropped to the floor, his pistol falling from the hand of a fast dying man.

'You're free to go, Marshal,' a stone-faced Bilby said. 'The shootin's over. When we start killin' each other it's a long way's over.'

He was slipping his pistol back into its holster when the Missourians rushed through the door, their pistols immediately covering him.

Billy had met up with Chuck and Joe partway along the street and told them that the red leg look-out had gone into a building just up ahead of them.

'That's where the bastards are holdin' Luther,' Chuck said. 'Now that all of them are off the street there's no need for us to be sneakin' along.'

The two pistol shots had them looking at each other before drawing their guns and racing along the street to Luther's aid.

158

'It's OK, boys,' Luther said. 'The captain's dead, shot by Mr Bilby there, the last of the red legs, just before the captain was going to plug me. The war is over at last. It's time for you to move on, go back to your farms and take up living again. Start by getting out of Plattsville, before the sheriff shows up and starts asking awkward questions. I'll stay and deal with him.'

Chuck broke the Missourians' silence once they had quickly weighed up Luther's advice. 'Put your guns away, boys,' he said. 'We'll do as the captain says and go home.' He looked at the tensed-up Bilby. 'Though I say this with no kindness in my heart, none of us will hinder you from goin' back to where you belong.'

Bilby gave the three Missourians a quick assaying glance. Judging that he had been told the truth, he gave his dead captain a final look and left the building by the back door.

'A wise decision, Chuck,' Luther said. 'And take Snake with you before the kid ends up swinging under some hanging tree.'

There was only time for curt goodbye nods before the Missourians started on their ride to their long neglected holdings. Luther armed up again and, his badge pinned to his shirt, walked out on to the street to meet the sheriff as one lawman to another. There was no sign of the sheriff hurrying along the boardwalk but he did see several men standing across the street eyeing him. He didn't know that the sheriff, sitting dozing in his office, had thought that the two shots were just firearms discharges by some drunken ranch hand or other, a regular occurence in Plattsville, so he stayed put. Luther thought that if the sheriff wasn't worrying about the shooting it wasn't his business to go along to his office and tell him about it. As from now he had quit being a peace officer. He took off his badge and stuffed it into his pocket.

Snake, leading two horses, met him before he reached the trees. He gave him a surprised look. 'I thought you. . . .'

Snake grinned. 'I'd never make a sodbuster, Luther.'

'You may not make much older if you stay in the Nations, Snake,' Luther replied. 'How does herding cattle suit you? I can fix you up with a job on the T Star. On the way to Texas we can swing by Jethro's place to tell him he'll never be bothered by red legs again.' Luther smiled slightly. 'M'be those two fine ladies will cook a meal for us before we leave?'

Snake thought of seeing the pretty Miss Betty Anne again, even though it would only be for a few minutes. But all his life his happy times hadn't run for any length of time. 'Boss,' he said, 'you've hired yourself a ranch hand!'

With some speed the pair rode west to reach Jethro's farm before nightfall.